Recipes for Disaster

Sheryl Browne

First published in 2012 by Safkhet Soul, Cambridge, United Kingdom
Safkhet Soul is an imprint of Safkhet Publishing

1 3 5 7 9 10 8 6 4 2

Text Copyright 2012 by Sheryl Browne
Recipe Text, Art and Photography Copyright 2012 by Kim Maya Sutton
Design Copyright 2012 Safkhet Publishing

Sheryl Browne asserts the moral right to be identified as the author of this work under the Copyright, Designs and Patents Act 1988.
Kim Maya Sutton asserts the moral right to be identified as the author of the recipe texts in this work, as well as the artist of the cover art and illustrations throughout this work under the Copyright, Designs and Patents Act 1988.

ISBN 978-1-908208-05-7

All characters and events in this publication, other than those clearly in the public domain, are fictitious and any resemblance to real persons, living or dead, is purely coincidental.

All rights reserved. No part of this publication may be reproduced, stored in or introduced into a retrieval system, or transmitted, in any form or by any means, including but not limited to electronic, mechanical, photocopying or recording, without the prior written permission of the publisher.

A CIP catalogue record for this book is available from the British Library.

Printed and bound by Lightning Source International

Typeset in 11 pt Crimson and Worstveld Sling Extra

Production Crew:
Sheryl Browne   *author*
Christina Hughes   *proofreader*
Mozart   *model (Rambo)*
Bryan E. Stachurski   *cover model*
Kim Maya Sutton   *artist, managing editor, recipe author, photographer*
William Banks Sutton *copy editor*

 The colophon of Safkhet is a representation of the ancient Egyptian goddess of wisdom and knowledge, who is credited with inventing writing. Safkhet Publishing is named after her because the founders met in Egypt.

A Note from Sheryl

Laughter for me is as essential as the air that we breathe and the food that we eat. Without it, every day would be a gray day. I'm a romcom writer, previously published in the US, and proud of it. Laughter, like an exquisite meal or a fine wine, makes people feel good. Escapism from the drudgery of life sometimes makes people read. And when we reach for our cookbook, we are similarly looking to escape the everyday drudge cooking can be. We want to create something tantalizingly different, delicious; artistic. We want to sit down with friends, to talk and laugh, impress a little; we want to escape.

What better then than combine delicious fun recipes with laugh-out-loud humor? Oh, and that all-essential ingredient: a sexilicious man? When Kim asked me, did I fancy a go at writing it, I thought WOW! Yes, please, swiftly followed by, God, but can I? As any writer will know, rite of passage rejections – though often accompanied by helpful suggestions, can take their toll. As a working mum and someone whose domestic Goddess gene really never did kick in (cue mumbles from son when girlfriend is invited to dinner, I want to kiss her not poison her), I wasn't sure I could measure up to the task.

I needn't have worried. Browsing Kim's recipes, I found myself smiling (yes, really. I have a mirror hiding a hole in the wall behind my computer). These recipes are fun, tummy-rumble inducing, inspiring. Why, even I fancied my chances at producing a gastronomic delight. Thus, my characters were born. And as I wrote, so it flowed. This book, I began to think, proudly, as my son – and biggest critic – laughed out loud while reading it, might not be the *Recipe for Disaster* I feared it could become, after all.

I'm thrilled to bits with the result. I've loved every minute of writing *Recipes for Disaster* and I hope you enjoy reading it and cooking from it half as much. If it makes you smile and you like my style, please watch this space www.sherylbrowne.com as I have other books coming soon. For writers, appreciative readers are always the most important ingredient.

Editor's Note

I wanted to write a cookbook that combines fun, recipes and black-and-white photography. When I received Sheryl's first inquiry letter, it occured to me that embedding the cookbook in a nice story would be a fantastic way to give you what you like most: inspiring recipes and fun when reading.

Before you can kick back, throw your legs on the coffee table, and indulge in the story with a nice glass of wine, however, there are a few things I'd like to point out.

The recipes in the book are my personal favorites, tried and true, and collected from very different parts of the world. I cook intuitively and propose you do the same. All recipes are in the imperial system, because I believe that's the more intuitive approach compared to immaculate metric measuring that suppresses your creativity. I realize that I cannot revolutionize the entire cooking world, so I want to give you metric cooks the chance to stick to your system.

All spoon measures are level unless otherwise specified.

1 tsp = 1 teaspoon = 5 ml;
1 tbsp = 1 tablespoon = 15 ml;
1 cup = 250 ml: this is a volume measurement. If you want to give my approach a try, find a cup, container or glass that holds 250 ml of water and then use that as your measuring device. Do not use 250 g of the listed ingredient instead of 1 cup; that will mess up your attempt at impressing Mr. (or Mrs.!) Right with tasty results.

A note on some ingredients...

If you are pregnant, avoid eating raw or lightly cooked eggs, poultry, meat, and unpasteurized cheeses. Use happy food (organic) when possible for best results. Please be aware that some recipes contain alcohol and do not consume these if you are pregnant or under age. If you zest (shred the peel) citrus fruits, use unwaxed, organic fruits.

Lastly, oven timings and temperatures are guides only, as individual ovens vary! You will just have to get to know yours. Make sure you test a recipe at least once before actually serving it to your aspired in-laws!

I'd like to thank Sheryl for giving this idea a go and writing what I think is exactly the right frame for the recipes. A big round of thanks also goes to Sheryl's family for the support they gave her: you've got a writing gem in your middle!

The thank you for the cover model cannot be outweighed with chocolate. He never knew he had such desirable, sexy legs until I pointed this hard-to-overlook-from-a-female-perspective-fact out. He then shyly agreed to posing in a pinny. Wouldn't be caught in said pinny outside of the office though, despite the light being better out there. We finally took the pictures in Safkhet's test kitchen and were all quite happy with the results. We owe you more than a dinner for this, Bryan!

William put his best effort into properly copy-editing and proofreading *Recipes for Disaster* while in stitches. I may just weigh myself in chocolate as a thank you for that.

Thank you to all you ladies and gentlemen who are reading this book now. We are already thinking of coming up with the next one, promise!

Humbly, I'd like to sneak in a thank you to all those who believe in us at Safkhet!

Dear reader, pour yourself a glass of wine, light a candle, put on Enrique Iglesias' *Enrique* (or whichever is *your* favorite romantic CD), lean back and enjoy *Recipes for Disaster* as we enjoyed putting it together.

Yours,

110°C	225°F	180°C	350°F
130°C	250°F	190°C	375°F
140°C	275°F	200°C	400°F
150°C	300°F	220°C	425°F
170°C	325°F	230°C	450°F

The Recipes

Starters
Cheese Cream Ahoi (Bavarian Cheese Cream) — page 129
Chilli Peppers (red pepper halves, filled with Chilli Con Carne; a twist on the traditional Texan dish) — page 24
Faith in Salad (a couscous, chicken and grape salad seemingly directly from Heaven, great in summer) — page 12

Soups
Green Soup (cold, green Gazpacho) — page 51
Red Soup (red beet soup, Borschtsch style) — page 35
White Soup (white asparagus cream soup) — page 72

Mains
Drunken Chicken (chicken in wine with green beans) — page 79
Olivia's Pride (vegetarian spinach lasagna, named after Popeye's girlfriend Olivia[1]) — page 57
Poseidon Serves Up (baked fish with seasonal vegetables) — page 131

Desserts
Frisian Anchor (red berry compote) — page 140
Peach Gobbler (peach cobbler, to gobble down) — page 106
Zebra (chocolate pudding with yoghurt) — page 91

Coffee Time
Cassata Seduction (an Italian cake-curd concoction) — page 43
Chockfull of Zucchinis (chocolate zucchini cake, great when you have too many zucchinis in your garden and nobody wants to see another glass of pickled zucches) — page 97
Pizza Cookie (a huge cookie, baked on a pizza sheet) — page 115

Select
Impress the In-Laws (avocado fudge) — page 65
Jammed in There (jam) — page 122
Stack O' Cakes (American-style stack of pancakes) — page 149

---

[1] I now know her name is *Olive Oyl*, but when I was a kid in Germany, I knew her as *Olivia* and thus originally called this dish Olivias Stolz.

For Drew

and all our loyal friends.

Chapter 1 Faith in Salad

"One cup red or green seedless grapes, three cups shredded chicken..."

"Okay, got it." Phone wedged between shoulder and earhole, I scribbled down the ingredients Becky was giving me — while frantically spraying Febreze to disguise the stench of dead fish.

"...cooked," Becky added.

"What?" I knitted my much furrowed brow.

"Three cups shredded... *cooked*... chicken." She spelled it out, slowly, as if talking to an incompetent. I might have taken umbrage, but for the fact that my domestic Goddess gene wasn't so much deficient, as it died, probably at birth. A slave in the kitchen I was not. Slut in the bedroom I could do. Or would quite like to. Somehow, though, I doubted the new man in my life would want to make mad passionate love to the girl who'd just killed off his mother.

"Honestly, Lisa..." Becky sighed. "It has to be cooked before you shred it. You can't shred raw chicken, can you?"

She was taking the pee now. "Obviously," I dripped, indignant, though there was a good possibility I might have tried.

"And make sure it's a happy chicken."

"*Ri-ght.*" I paused to ponder. "Cooked and shredded, I should think it'll be highly amused."

"Oh, ha-di-ha." Becky didn't sound impressed. "I meant, an organic chicken, plucked and without giblets. Wash it under cold water, then place the whole chicken in a big pot, cover it with water, and bring it to a boil over a high heat."

"By which time it will be positively ecstatic."

Silence.

"Ahem. High heat, got you. Go on."

"Make sure it doesn't boil over," Becky continued, after an audible *humph*. "Once it's boiling, you can turn down the heat. Let the bird cook for at least one hour and then check if it comes off the bone easily. If not, turn off the heat and leave it in the pot until it does. Depending on the size of the bird, this might take a bit longer."

"Becky, slow down!" I scrawled frenziedly and tried to keep up. "Right, got it. I think. Next?"

Becky emitted another despairing sigh. "Order a takeaway."

"Sorry?"

"Never mind." She sighed — again, pointedly. "Repeat back what I've just said."

"Hold on." I turned to kick the back door closed before I got frostbite, then grabbed up the saucepan containing the culinary catastrophe I might have poisoned new man Adam and his mom with — and tipped it in the dog dish.

Then padded back across the kitchen and fell over the dog.

"Ooh, God! *Three cups shredded cooked... absolutely delighted... chicken!*" I snapped, straightening up from the work surface, which mercifully broke my fall before I parted company with my teeth. "Good boy, Rambo," I cooed, more sweetly. "Din dins, hon."

My midget Jack Russell looked at me, looked at the dish — wherein floated a monkfish head, sniffed it, curled a lip, I would swear, then beat a hasty retreat to the hall.

"What else?" I asked after the next ingredient, while heaving out a sigh of my own, then trying hard not to breathe back in. The Bouillabaisse — traditional Provençal fish stew (*Easy Fish* recipe book now in trash) — I'd decided to serve for the brunch Adam had invited himself and his mother to, smelled horribly pungent while cooking. Burned, it could strip the lining from your lungs. I shudder to think what it would do to your digestive tract.

"Patience, lots of... on my part," Becky went on wearily, "one cup thinly sliced celery, half a cup thinly sliced green onions, half a cup chopped, salted roasted pistachios..."

"Pistachios?! Where am I supposed to get..."

"Kitchen cupboard, right hand side. At least, that's where they were at Christmas."

"Oh, right." I nodded and wondered whether I should also do an inventory of my kitchen cupboards... sometime.

"Next..." Becky went on efficiently: "...a quarter cup of fresh chopped mint leaves. And, yes, you have got some," she assured me. "You bought it when you got the parsley and thyme for the Bouillabaisse. You'll also need... two cups cooked couscous. If you like, you can use Bulgur or rice instead."

"Is that it?" I asked, feeling overwhelmed by the task ahead as well as odious smells.

"For the salad, yes. For the *Curry Chutney Dressing*, you'll need..." Tescos, I thought wanly.

"...three quarters of a cup of non-fat yogurt, a quarter cup mayonnaise, three teaspoons chopped mango chutney, one teaspoon curry powder, a quarter teaspoon each cayenne pepper and salt"

"Salt? Salt?! I haven't got any frickin' salt, have I? That's what caused all the trouble in the first place. 'A pinch of salt' the recipe for the soup said. And what happens? What could only happen to me? The top plops off, that's what. And then — whoosh — I have fish-flavored salt! And what does the online Recipe Rescue site say? Increase all the other ingredients. I now have enough soup to feed the Salvation Army — and it tastes foul!"

"All right. All right, calm down," Becky said. "It's not the end of the world."

"It *is*," I wailed, stuffing my face in the fridge in search of yogurt and mayo. "What didn't spew out all over the stove is burned to the bottom of the saucepan. It smells awful, like sweaty feet. The canary keeled over and fell off its perch; the dog's crawled under the hall cupboard and... Oh, *hell*...now the flipping smoke alarm's gone into overdrive."

Still muttering, I headed for the utility cupboard and the broom I kept handy for just such occasions — of which there were many — to give the shrieking alarm a good jab.

"It's a quarter teaspoon, Lisa. There'll be more than enough in the salt shaker." Becky informed me pseudo-patiently, as silence ensued.

"Oh, yes, well... thank you." I sucked in a necessary breath and marched back to the kitchen, shoulders determinedly back and girds loined... loins girded... something anyway.

"Only *you* could burn soup," Becky observed helpfully.

The shoulders drooped. Unbelievable. I plucked my phone from under my chin and glared at it. I could just see her, my so-called best friend and master-chef extraordinaire, rolling her perfectly made-up eyes and examining her immaculate nail extensions, no doubt while her espresso brewed and her home-baked pastries browned. "Yes," I said, slitty-eyed with accusation, "and *you* know I can burn soup. And it's all *your* fault."

"*My* fault?"

"Yes, yours."

Becky huffed. "Oh, well, if you're going to..."

"*You* told him I could cook."

"*You* put the M&S boxes in the trash." Becky's voice went up an octave.

"Well, what else would I do with them? Hang them on the Christmas tree?"

"You could have said something," Becky argued. "Admitted it was haute cuisine care of Saint Michael you were serving, instead of smiling coyly and fluttering your eyelashes."

I opened my mouth and closed it. Becky was right. The thing was that I'd been expecting her to turn up with some spotty geek with a personality bypass in tow. It had been my turn to cremate the pre-Christmas lunch this year. Every year we, the curry girls, who meet once a month at *The Dilshad* to eat a lot and catch up on the goss, have a pre-Christmas get-together at one or another of our homes — with partners. I hadn't got one. A partner, that was, not a home. And I didn't mind. I'd decided I'd rather cuddle my dog than be dumped again for some slim, young thing with Botox brow, breast implants and panache in the kitchen. Becky, on the other hand, had been on a mission, if not to fix me up with a mate for life, to at least get me back in the dating game. It was my interests she'd had at heart, I know. I'd been a bit of a recluse since being dumped, missing several girly nights in a row. It wasn't the dumping that had pulverized my own heart; it was the miscarriage two weeks afterwards.

That had been six months prior though, and I'd come to the conclusion Becky might be right. It was time to pull myself together, pick out my best dress and say yes. I only had to talk to the guy, who Becky had said was a bit lonely. I did quietly hope she'd turn up with Colin Firth in a wet shirt, I must admit, but my hopes weren't high.

And then she'd walked in with Adam. And as cuddly and kissable as my little Rambo is, there was frankly no contest. Adam was gorgeous, tall, dark, dreamy chocolate-brown eyes, shy smile: killer combination. Adam was also a policeman it turned out — and the thought of a uniform with him in it. Scratchy blue serge next to my skin... I'd fluttered like mad.

Adam, it also turned out, was a widower. Well, that was it. My heart melted.

From the way he looked when he spoke briefly of her, I knew he'd loved his wife. A small part of him might always, I supposed, since they hadn't done what mutually parting couples do and fallen out of love. That was okay. I couldn't resent her. But I did, human traits being what they are. Adam's wife, I learned, was an excellent cook.

The secret of Saint Michael never did come out.

"Sorry," I mumbled, idly doodling on my recipe list.

FAITH IN SALAD
1 cup red or green seedless grapes
3 cups shredded cooked... happy (!!!) chicken
1 cup thinly sliced celery

"S'okay. I know you're a bit stressed," Becky said kindly. "Look, I'll email you the cooking instructions; give you a chance to sort yourself out. Or are you going to go back to being recluse and hide under the blanket?"

"Blanket." My mouth twitched upwards. "With Adam with a bit of luck."

"Right, well, you'd better get his mom on side, then. Have faith, hon; excuse the pun. You can do this."

"Ye-es." Becky's faith, I suspected, might be a little misplaced.

The table was set. I had five minutes to make myself gorgeous. I glanced in the hall mirror. No problem. A head-transplant should do it.

Ugh. His mom's half-French, apparently, on her mother's side (thus the biliousness-inducing Bouillabaisse) and bound to be elegant and stylish. Me, I'm right on trend — not — squeezed into leggings that make my derriere look like a barrage balloon and a New Look top mislabeled size fourteen instead of age fourteen. Desperate, I flew up to my bedroom, Rambo panting after me, only to turn-rapid-tail at the bedroom door. Clever little JR, he knew better than to get underfoot in the danger zone. Ooh, no. The *hair*! I blinked forlornly at my reflection, flicking the straighteners on with one hand and slicking lipstick on with the other. I have *that* kind of hair. Strawberry blonde, naturally wavy, scary hair. Two minutes I told myself, willing the clock hands to stay still, while squeezing a single droplet of serum, or six million... *Aaargh*! ...into the palm of my hand. Why does this keep happening?!

"Damn." I rubbed palms together, wiped the excess on a pair of panties in the absence of anything else to hand, ran gunk through my frizz-ends, then... "Doh."

Ding dong went the doorbell.

Splat went my heart, plummeting swiftly to the soles of my feet.

Hell! Plucking up the straighteners, I swept them through one side and then the other, then — sizzling a bit — bowled out of the bedroom.

"Coming," I trilled. "Rambo, sweetie, come here, hon." Thundering downstairs, I tried to attract the attention of the miniature Rottweiler, who'd just splatted himself against the front door.

"Rambo..." Trying to keep my tone that of a kind-to-animals-kind-of-person, I tried again, "...come on, baby. Come into the living room with Mommy, hmm?"

I jiggled excitedly in that direction.

"*Rrrowf, rrrowf. Yeah, rrright,*" went Rambo, little front legs bouncing off the floor with gusto.

"Rambo!"

"*Pant, pant,*" went Rambo, zipping niftily left when I tried to grab him, then right, pointy ears straight up, stump wagging frenziedly — and then piddling all over me, as I plucked him up.

Finally, Rambo Rottie wriggling underarm, manic smile fixed in place, I grappled the door open. "Adam!" I exclaimed delightedly.

"*RRRRooWF*," said Rambo. Wriggle. Piddle.

"Oh," said the coiffed, designer-dressed woman on my doorstep, looking my-sad-self up and down, obviously unimpressed.

OhmiGod, it's the Queen. I gulped quietly. Helen Mirren at her all-time hoity-toity best.

"He-lloo," I sing-songed cheerily. "You must be..."

"His mother," she announced, less a greeting, more a threat.

"Right, well, lovely to meet you. Do come in." My smile less enthusiastic, but still plastered in place nevertheless, I pulled the door wide and stood aside.

"He's parking the car," Her Royal Haughtiness informed me snootily, stepping inside and sniffing the air.

Oh, please God, she'd detected fragrance of Febreze, not odor of fish — or worse, pee.

Panicking inside and feeling utterly tongue-tied, I looked out for signs of rescue. And it came, the man of my dreams, even if he did have a nightmare mother.

"Hi, gorgeous," he said, smiling his bone-melting smile as he hurried toward the house. Ooh, he was sooo sexy. And in his uniform, he could have any flesh-and-blood female panting without even removing his cap. He could certainly have me.

"Sorry," he mouthed, looking sheepish as he apologized again for bringing his mother — whose idea it was to pop in and see his new girlfriend. They'd almost be passing the door, apparently, on the way to his aunt's, from where she would be going to the hospital to undergo a knee operation the next morning. This meal was to be her last, Adam had said. Little did he know how chilling a prophecy that almost was.

I gave him a reassuring smile. It wasn't really Adam's fault. I had to meet her sometime, I'd supposed. Might have been nice to smother him in chocolate sauce and eaten him for dessert before failing the mother test though.

Adam widened his smile, his sultry brown eyes liquefying me from tummy to toes as he leaned in for a kiss, then stopped and cocked his head to one side. "New perfume?" he asked, his expression bemused.

"Dog pee," I said, dipped and sidestepped. Oh, I wanted to kiss him, thoroughly, but sucking on his tongue I reckoned mightn't be prudent with his mother looking on.

"Ah, hunter, killer's been at it again, then? Hi, Rambo." He stroked

Rambo's head, who bared his tiny needle-like teeth and growled. "I think he's warming to me." Adam laughed.

True, I thought, as Rambo plopped out of my arms. He'd tried to bite Adam last time, but at least he didn't... "Rambo, kitchen!" I said, as he made a beeline for HRH's shoes, back leg twitching and looking suspiciously as if he might pee on her peep toes.

Rambo glanced back at me. As if, said the look, then he turned to do his hard-man swagger to the cat flap in the back door.

"Mom, this is Lisa," Adam made the introductions as his mother watched Rambo go, most definitely unimpressed now. "Lisa, my mom."

"Pleased to meet you." I stopped short of the curtsy and extended my hand. His mom looked down at it as if it were a tentacle, then remembered she too had hands. "Isabelle," she said, offering one at length, but not for long.

"Right, well, I thought we'd, um, eat in the, um..." I nodded toward the kitchen, where was my dining area, furnished with an ancient Ikea table and mismatching chairs, ditto the cushions. I'd tried to kid myself it was shabby-chic, but now I felt it was just shabby. "Would anyone like to, um...?"

I shrugged hopelessly at this point, as Isabelle stared at the oil slick on her hand and then at her son. And I could read that look. Horrified to meet me, obviously.

Ooh, this was awful. I should never have agreed to it. Never. At least not until I'd done a cookery course, had a make-over and redecorated the whole house. Dejectedly, I led the way into the kitchen, as Her Maj went to avail herself of the toilet. Heck, had I flushed it? Was there any toilet paper? Should I tap on the door, I wondered, and offer her some kitchen paper? No, probably not. My shoulders drooped. Then perked up a bit when Adam placed his arm around them.

"Thanks," he said, pulling me to him to plant a soft kiss on my lips. "She can be a pain sometimes, but she's really worried about this op. Especially after Melissa..." He stopped there, smiling apologetically, again. I didn't want him to do that, to feel he had to apologize for mentioning his wife. She'd existed. He'd lost her after she'd had a stay in hospital, it seemed. I didn't want him to feel awkward every time her name might come up.

I definitely didn't want to feel awkward every time her name came up. Her Maj hadn't got as far as parking her posh posterior on my shabby cushion, when she mentioned his wife for a second time.

"Well, doesn't this all look… nice," she said, sweeping her eyes cursorily over the table, then checking the cushion before lowering herself cautiously onto it. "Melissa was a wonderful cook, of course, wasn't she, Adam?"

My heart sank. Okay, so it might not be the Cordon Bleu her refined palate was used to, but it looked pretty, carefully arranged on each plate. As per the instructions, I'd made a little impression in the couscous, filled it with shredded chicken, covered it lovingly with salad and surrounded the ring with dressing. And I'd made absolutely sure to pluck all the bits of inadvertently added bone out.

She'd first mentioned her when she'd walked into the kitchen. Melissa had decorated her downstairs toilet in the exact same wallpaper I had in my living room, apparently. She'd peeked in there then — impudent cow — and was making a huge point, I felt.

Adam looked really awkward now. Raking a hand through his hair, he blew out a sigh, then reached for my hand under the table and gave it a squeeze. I squeezed his hand gently back, and then almost snapped his fingers off. My eyes boggled, then nearly fell out and rolled away. There through the cat flap came Rambo's bottom, which I'd thought was a bit odd. But then, Jack Russells are feisty, entertaining little dogs, always up to new tricks. He was probably dragging a soggy soft-toy in from the garden, I'd first thought.

Oh, no, not Rambo. Rambo entertained big style. His stumpy tail appeared, his rump appeared, he wriggled backward with a frustrated growl, then tugged and heaved… a dead monkfish-head through the flap, complete with pupils.

Help! I gagged on the perfectly crisped French stick I'd popped in my mouth. Then, in an inspiring moment of crisis-deflecting madness, spat it out.

"Sorry," I croaked, as all eyes turned to me, rather than the flat-eyed fish being dragged slowly across the kitchen floor. "Asthma." I pressed a hand to my chest and croaked some more. And wheezed. And scooped the offending French missile into my napkin (kitchen paper).

"Asthma?" Adam looked alarmed. He placed a hand on my back, softly massaging, caring... His sultry brown eyes were full of concern. God love him. I'm sure I was beginning to. I so wished he would carry me caringly into bed and massage me all over.

"I'm fine," I assured him, feeling terribly guilty. He really did look worried. "I only get the odd attack when I get stressed." That bit wasn't a lie. I did have an inhaler, but didn't often use it.

"Yes, well, I'm not surprised you're feeling stressed..." Adam shot his mother a look of utter despair "...under the circumstances."

He passed me some water.

I sipped.

Isabelle shifted on her cushion.

Nobody said a word.

Disaster.

It was all ruined. They would go. They'd probably have words. Or have no words, like now. And then he'd feel guilty because she was going into hospital. And *she* would hate me. Stick little pins in an effigy of me probably.

I swallowed. I felt like crying.

Oh hell. I hoisted the shoulders up. I intended to enjoy my hard-worked-at brunch, even if Lady Muck did sit there looking grim. "Well, *bon voyage*," I said, determinedly plucking up my fork.

Adam glanced at me, mouthed, "Sorry," again, and did likewise. Isabelle looked haughtily down her nose at her plate, then noting the stern look Adam was now giving her, followed suit.

"There's more *Curry Chutney Dressing*." I nodded at the dish center-table. "It makes a wonderful spread for leftover chicken-topped baguettes," I gabbled on, desperate to fill the ensuing silence. So the recipe instructions suggest, I didn't elaborate. "But I can always whip up some more. Enjoy!"

I stuffed a mouthful of my *Faith in Salad* in my mouth, prayed to God Becky's faith in my ability to produce it paid off, tried not to wish fervently his mother choked on hers, and made up my mind I would damn well enjoy it.

"It's all homemade, then?" Isabelle asked, popping a tentative forkful daintily into her mouth.

"Yes." I nodded, stuffing another hearty forkful into mine.

"Really?" Adam looked incredulous.

"Yes." I chomped and tried not to spit couscous. "Why?"

"Nothing," Adam shook his head. "Just... it's good."

Oh. I paused to savor. "Yes, it is, isn't it?" I agreed, with a modest little smile. OohmiGosh, I thought. Mmmmm. Yess! Yesss. *Yessss*! I'm a Goddess!

"Very. *Bon appétit.*" Adam grinned, licked a fleck of dressing from the side of his mouth with the tip of his tongue and gave me a look I couldn't quite read. "I'll be back for seconds," he promised, with a slow wink.

Now *that* look, I could read. Sexilicious. I sighed, replete, almost.

"Ye-es." Isabelle contemplated, at length "Very more... ish," she said, a smile cracking her frozen face as she shoved in a full forkful. "You must give me the recipe."

"Absolutely." I nodded, munched happily, and tried to resist biting Adam.

"Here you go: the recipe," I announced, fetching the cooking instructions, which Becky — true to her word — had emailed, allowing me time to clear up evidence of failed fish soup. Speaking of which, where had Rambo gone with his dead-head of one?

Faith in Salad

Ingredients for 4 portions:

3 cups shredded, cooked chicken

2 cups cooked couscous (bulgur or rice can be substituted, depending on preference and larder content)

Salad:

1 cup red or green seedless grapes

1 cup thinly sliced celery

½ cup thinly sliced green onions

½ cup chopped, salted, roasted pistachios

¼ cup fresh mint leaves, finely chopped

Curry Chutney Dressing:

¾ cup non-fat yogurt

¼ cup mayonnaise

3 tsp chopped mango chutney

1 tsp curry powder

¼ tsp cayenne pepper

¼ tsp salt

First of all, make sure you actually buy a happy chicken. Organic is best, plucked, and without giblets. Bring it home and wash it under cold water. Place the whole chicken in a big pot and cover it with water. Put the lid on the pot and bring to a boil over high heat. You do want to be somewhere nearby so it does not boil over. Once boiling, you can turn down the heat. The bird needs to cook for at least one hour, but not rapidly. You can test the meat by checking if it comes off the bones easily. Once it does, it's done. If it doesn't after one hour, just turn the heat off and let it sit there in its pot until it does. Depending on the size of the bird, this may take a bit longer than one hour.

If you feel like you cannot wait for this, buy a few organic chicken breasts and cook them covered in water for about 20 minutes until they can be easily shredded.

Whichever option you choose, in the meantime, you can cut the grapes, celery, green onions, pistachios and mint leaves, and mix that all together in a bowl.

For the dressing, mix all the listed ingredients and let stand.

Depending on your preference, prepare couscous, bulgur or rice. For couscous or bulgur, you will want to use about 1 cup dry couscous (or bulgur). Bring 2 cups of water to a boil (use a kettle, that's fastest and the most convenient), pour this over the couscous (or bulgur) and let stand. That's all you need to do! If you want to use rice, cover 1 cup of rice in 2 cups of water, bring to a boil, turn off the stove, and place a lid on the rice after 5 minutes of cooling off. Let sit on the warm stove (if you are using a gas stove, leave the fire on the tiniest flame you've got). After about 20 minutes, your rice will be perfect.

The chicken is probably done now. If you used a whole chicken, take it out of the hot water, but keep the water (this will make a perfect soup base for the next day). Let the chicken cool a while, so you can touch it. Peel the chicken off the bones and throw the bones away. Do not give them to your dog; dogs should never eat chicken bones! Shred the chicken as you go along. Measure 3 cups and keep the rest for a sandwich or soup for the next day. If you are using chicken breasts, shred the meat after cooking it. If it is too hot to touch, use two forks.

To assemble the salad and plate it up, put out the four plates you want to use. Place one fourth of the couscous, bulgur, or rice on each plate. Make a small impression in it and fill with one fourth of the shredded chicken. Cover with one fourth of the salad and surround the ring with the dressing. Voilà!

For the next day, you can use the broth you kept, add some remaining chicken and cut up 2 cups of whatever vegetables you have in the house (carrots, celery, parsnips, potatoes, eggplant, zucchini, peppers, …). Re-heat this and simmer (lightly cook) for 10 to 15 minutes and you have the perfect quick chicken soup.

Or you can place the remaining chicken and some of the dressing (if you have any leftover) on a baguette and you'll have a wonderful chicken salad sandwich with which to impress your loved one.

I hastily scanned the hall as I showed them out. The decapitated fish skull was nowhere in evidence. The smell, however, was. Isabelle's nose twitched a bit as she searched around for her shoulder bag.

"Ah, here it is." She retrieved it from where she'd left it, on the bottom step of the stairs. "A pleasure to meet you, my dear," she said, air-kissing my cheek then turning to the front door, which Adam was holding for her, being a good son.

"We'll get together vis-à-vis the Ladies Golf Club do. I'll ring you," Isabelle promised, flapping her recipe behind her as she took her leave. She wants me to help her cater for it, haw, haw. Ooh, er.

"Okey, dokey." I smiled wanly and waved her off.

"Back soon," Adam said huskily, gave me an orgasm-inducing, slow, sexy smile and followed his mother out.

Dutiful hostess, I watched them down the path, waited patiently while Isabelle fumbled her bag from her shoulder to put her recipe inside for safekeeping. Then closed it post-haste when she peered pale-faced inside it and screamed.

"Rambo?!"

Chapter 2 Spice up Your Love Life

Determined to reciprocate after the trouble Lisa had gone to... Okay, desperate to move things on, despite my mother's haughty reservations and Lisa's midget-Rottweiler's determination to hinder my attempts, I grabbed up a shopping basket, walked boldly into unchartered territory — and fell at the first fence. Having had a mother who could cook, and a wife, ditto... Well, I just hadn't, embarrassingly. Puzzled, I read the first ingredient again.

Four poblano peppers. Erm, so what are poblano peppers, exactly? (If you can't find those, bell peppers or any other 5-6 inch long mild pepper can be substituted). Ahh... Nope. Still clueless. Wandering toward the fruit and veg, I scanned the wares on display. *Peppers? Peppers?* Ah, peppers! All manner of. Which helps... not. Frowning, I studied the labels, then gave up and asked the woman next to me. "Cooking for my girlfriend," I explained, trying not to look too inept. Her knowing smile — as in knowing an inept man when she saw one — widened and she pointed out the poblano peppers, which were hidden right under my nose, "pronounced *puh blah noh*," she informed me confidently.

Thanking her, I stored the information away with which to impress Lisa, and read on: one pound ground meat (whichever is preferred, half pork and half beef is best, but it's cook's choice). Pork, I decided. Go the whole hog, why not. I headed purposefully for the meat counter, then turned back.

One jalapeño (or other hot pepper; more if you like it hot) was next on the list. Followed by: 1 shallot, 1 garlic clove, 4 plum tomatoes, ½ cup of cheese (again, cook's preference: cheddar, mozzarella, gouda,...), salt, freshly ground black pepper, 1 tsp olive oil, and 1 cup fresh mixed herbs (a combination of basil, tarragon, oregano, parsley, rosemary).

Which meant it made sense to stick with the fruit and veg section. Promoting myself in the competence department, I found the jalapeño, closely followed by the shallot and garlic clove. I was getting good at this. Maybe I could be a professional shopper instead of a copper? It might even pay more.

Now then, plum tomatoes? Ah, yep, knew where they were. Next to the beans. I set forth for the tinned aisle, and then stopped. Or did they come fresh? I doubled back, pausing in front of an array of tomatoes. Cripes. Well, they weren't in short supply, unlike my savvy shopping skills. So which were the... "Er, excuse me?" I spotted a shop assistant, who immediately sped off in the opposite direction. "Plum tomatoes?" I asked hopefully, cutting her off before she gave me the slip.

"Tinned or fresh?"

"Good question." I showed her my list.

Sighing audibly, she turned to march back to the fruit and veg, me trailing behind, hard-pushed to keep up. Stopping back at the tomatoes, she gave me a 'typical man' look, then, "Plum tomatoes. They're plum-shaped," she pointed out, reproachfully.

"Right." I smiled. "In disguise, then. Probably trying to avoid being chopped up and cooked."

Nope, she wasn't amused, I gathered, as she wandered off, wearing a save-me-from-stupid-shoppers look. Fearing my incompetence might be about to be hailed over the loudspeaker, I managed to work out which little green leaves were which by myself, and, mixed herbs selected, headed off for the pork. Cheese, ground pepper and olive oil also accomplished unaided, I zipped over to the wine section and selected a robust red, then went back for a Sauvignon Blanc. Not sure what Lisa's preferences were wine-wise, I wanted everything to be perfect.

The bottom dropping out of a shopping bag before I got through the front door didn't bode well. "*Grrreat.* Frickin' things!" I dumped the other bags and went back for the spilled contents.

"*Grrreat.*" Flint squawked, from his perch in the living room. "*Frickin' things. Caw, caw. Grrrea...*"

"Flint, zip it! Or you're up on eBay," I threatened, irked by his chirpiness, despite my squashed plum tomato predicament. I'd have to cover him up. My efforts at wooing Lisa with good food and soft lighting, I reckoned might be a bit hampered by a neurotic, balding parrot, flapping its wings and croaking, "*Who's a clever boy then?*"

Flint was a present from Mel. Personally, I'd have preferred an iPhone but, having confessed I'd accidentally Scotchgarded my budgie while spraying my boots, she'd got it into her head I needed a replacement to help me over the trauma. It was pretty traumatic at the time, though at seventeen, I couldn't admit to my pals I was upset. I pretended an urgent call of nature instead. Crying over a weather-protected but well-dead budgie just wouldn't have been considered macho.

I collected the tomatoes up, along with the *poh Blah* pepper, wiped a few splotches off it, and hurried back in — to find the telephone ringing.

Oh, no. I groaned. Mom, it had to be. "Perfect frickin' timing, as per." What did she want now? Frustrated, I picked up. She was still on crutches, I reminded myself guiltily. And she had only rung me three times since I'd left her this morning.

"Hi, Mom. How's…"

"*Perfect frickin' timing. Caw, caw. Perfect,*" Flint mimicked from the living room, followed by a perfect imitation of the vacuum,

"Flint, one more word and *you* are stuffed," I growled aside.

"*Clever boy.*" Flint nutted his bell, obviously pleased at his wit.

"Mom. How are you doing?" I went back to the phone, praying this wasn't an emergency, i.e. she'd run out of gin to go with her tonic.

There was a loaded pause on the other end, followed by, "Much better for knowing you care, darling."

Oh, God, not the 'darling'. Darling — accompanied by a stoic sniff — was more an accusation than a term of endearment. *I love you dearly, would lay down my life for you — as only a mother would — but I can manage without you… when I need you… if you're too busy…*

"Mom…" I sighed, exasperated. "I do care. You know I do, but…"

"You have better things to do, I know," she finished woefully.

"*Things* to do, Mom, yes." I tried not to sound too impatient.

"Such as entertaining Lucy."

"Lisa, Mom, as you very well know. And, yes, I am. I like her, Mom. I…" I stopped, not inclined to discuss my love life — or lack thereof — with my mother.

"I gathered," Mom said sniffily, which translated *though I have no idea why*. The thing is, Mom wants me to be happy, but happy in her mind means finding someone who exactly replicates Melissa. She wants me to move on, but she doesn't want to let go, probably because she and Mel got on so well, mostly because Mel was a fabulous cook — specialty French cuisine, which had her on a par with a Goddess in

Mom's opinion. I loved Mel, but in my mind, in my heart, I felt in order to move on, *I* had to let go. I would never forget her, how could I? I would always be grateful for the good times we had, but I didn't want memories of Mel to color my future relationships. Mel hadn't wanted that either. She'd made me promise to love again, though it almost choked me. No, I could never forget my wife, the almost mother of my children, but after two years... Well, meeting Lisa brought home hard the loneliness of being alone. Lisa had made me smile, made me feel okay to be me, no history. It was time to make new memories, hopefully with Lisa.

"I suppose she does have a certain something," Mom conceded, then paused, as if considering what. "At least she can cook."

A small plus in her favor, then? I was getting seriously annoyed now. "But..."

"But what, Mom?" I asked tersely.

"Just promise me you'll be careful tonight, Adam."

"Erm..." *Frickin' hell.* Talk about Mother's beady eye on me. She'd turned into a mind reader.

"Don't forget the fish head", she expounded gravely.

I stifled a laugh. "I won't," I promised. "If I wake up to a horse head in the bed, I'll let you know."

"Adam!"

Crap. Perhaps I shouldn't have mentioned the bed bit.

"It's no joking matter. It was a very... peculiar thing to do."

Yeah, but hilarious, I felt it better not to point out. "Rambo dropped it there, Mom, not Lisa. She's not a closet psychopath."

"*Ye-es.*" Mother didn't sound convinced. "Still, just be careful, darling. You don't really know her that well, do you?"

"No, but I'd like to." I sighed wistfully.

"Sorry?"

"Nothing. Did you want something, Mom? It's just... *tempus fugit,* you know?"

"No, no. Don't you worry about me, dah-ling," she said, this time with a breeziness she knew very well *I knew* was forced. "I had a little fall, that's all, but..."

What?! "Well why didn't you...? I'm on my way."

"...I'm fine," she said, as I was half out the door. "A bit shaken, obviously, but I managed to scrape myself up from the floor... eventually."

Jesus. I sucked in a breath. Was she? "You're sure?" I asked warily.

"Of course. A bit bruised, but nothing a painkiller won't fix. Honestly, Adam, you do worry too much, you know?"

I sighed wearily. "I wonder why."

"Go on, you get off and have a lovely evening with Lucy. Don't you concern yourself about me... being on my own. I'm perfectly capable."

"Right." I blew out a sigh. "I'll try not to." Promising to call in on her the next morning, I finally got off the phone with... "*Christ.*"...forty minutes to rustle up haute cuisine.

"Dammit!" I dove to the kitchen, Flint squawking, "*Christ. Dammit!*" hilariously behind me.

Right ingredients assembled, I diced the shallot, covered it in ground pepper and put it to one side. Next I peeled the garlic — once I'd found my way into it, before cutting that into small pieces. The instructions did suggest I could use a garlic press if preferred. Being not totally incompetent, I did know what a garlic press was, but how to use it...? An Xbox needs putting together, I'm your man. The garlic press, however, was a gadget beyond me.

Finding a pan fit for the job, I splashed in the olive oil, then, while that was warming over a medium heat, I washed and cut the jalapeño into tiny pieces, including seeds.

Right, thumb still intact and hands washed, I chucked the garlic, meat and jalapeño into the pan to fry slowly until lightly browned and crumbly. Frickin' good this. I could open a restaurant. Whistling while I worked, I set the oven to pre-heat to 350°F, boiled the kettle for a quick coffee, then — "S*quaaaawk*" — missed my mouth and tipped it all over me. "*Shi... ooot!* That is hot!

Urgency dictating, I opted for jeans first and stripped the lot off, including boxers. *Phew.* A bit pink in places, but no permanent damage, thank God. First aid cream liberally applied might look a bit iffy. Tugging off my T-shirt, I headed for the washer, hoping Lisa might be the slightest bit impressed by what was underneath. Was chest hair in or out? Did Lisa go for guys with chest hair? Maybe I should fish a bit over the *poh blah*? Yeah, right, and then excuse myself to... what? Pluck them out?

Ah, well, too late now. And wasn't I getting just the tiniest bit ahead of myself? The last thing I wanted was for Lisa to...

Drrriiing went the doorbell.

...arrive early?

"*Hell!*" Panic-struck, I grabbed the pinny from a hook on the door — pulled it on, and, "Perfect." Not. A naked-lady-adorned-pinny wasn't really desired attire to greet one's girlfriend in, I suspected.

"Crap!" I searched desperately for inspiration, and found — the hand-towel. It would have to do. Wrapping it around my midriff, holding it firm at the back, I headed up the hall, pulled in a breath, and swung the door wide. "Lisa." I smiled, trying to look clever, in a master chef sort of way.

"Adam?" she said, looking me curiously up and down.

"I was just, erm…" I waved toward the kitchen "…preparing…"

"*Crrraaap!*" Flint squawked behind me.

"…stuffed parrot," I grated.

Lisa's frowned. "Sorry?"

"Peppers. Stuffed. Would you like to, er…?" I gestured her in.

"Um…" Lisa hesitated. "No. I, um…"

"Oh." My heart plummeted to about towel level.

"Becky…" Lisa's gaze travelled to towel level. "She, um…"

"Ahem." I coughed awkwardly, extremely.

Lisa's gaze twanged back to mine. "She's in the car." She indicated her car, where Becky sat, her eyes agog, fingers waving daintily.

"I was giving her a lift on the way," Lisa went on, her eyes now fixed firmly on my face. Beautiful eyes. Emerald green, pupils like saucers. Beautiful lips, ripe for tasting. Christ, how I wanted to pull her into my arms… arm, the only one I had available… and kiss her senseless right there on the…

"But Rambo was sick in her lap."

"Oh?" That spoiled the mood a bit, I have to admit. I tore my attention away from Lisa's kissable lips and down to the two-inch German shepherd at her feet.

"I wondered whether I could leave him with you." Lisa plucked him up.

"Ahh, right." Relief flooded through me, closely followed by a fresh bout of panic, as Lisa thrust the dog toward me, which was less to do with the needle-sharp teeth Rambo was baring, more to do with the bits I would be if I took him.

Lisa obviously noted my reluctance. "He's fine now," she assured me. "He gets a bit travel sick, don't you, poor baby, hmm?" She kissed the top of his furry head, then plucked up a paw and kissed his toes. There may be hope for my hairy chest yet.

"Fine, no problem," I said. "Do you want to just... drop him? I, erm, jalapeño," I improvised, "on my hands. Don't want him to get it in his eyes."

"Bless." Lisa blinked at me bemusedly, then she stood up on tiptoe and brushed her sweet lips against mine. "You're lovely," she said.

Well, that perked me up a bit.

"I know. And modest." I smiled and leaned forward to steal another kiss, then stopped, distracted by a muffled grumble lower down.

"*Grrrowf.*" Rambo imparted his thoughts on my kissing his mistress. "*Grrrrowf.*" Wriggle. "*Grrrrrr.*"

"Oooh, sweetie!" Lisa cuddled him, cheek-to-cheek. "Was Mommy squishing you, hmm?"

"*Rrrowf.*" Baby wagged his stump, gave me a look, which roughly read *piss off dude*, then licked her, tongue to mouth. Er, okay. I'm not prudish. I don't mind a bit of dog slobber. "*Rrrrowf.*"

Dog pee, however, ... I sighed and eyed the skies.

Rambo was barking with gusto up at Flint when I passed the living room. "*Rrrowf, rrrowf,*" he went, front feet bouncing off the floor, then panting around in a circle and going at it some more.

Flint peered down at him, a long way down, nutted his bell, then let rip with a *Rrrroowwwf* that froze Rambo mid-bounce and made his fur stand on end.

"Met your match, hey, Stallone? Serves you right, rat-dog." I smirked, as legs like propellers, Rambo's hindquarters disappeared into the kitchen, then, "*Shoot,* the pan!" I skidded after him. *Phew.* I rescued the pork, before it was burnt to a crisp, then, turning to slam the washing machine door and wham the machine on, I headed upstairs to slip into something more comfortable.

All was eerily quiet when I came back down. "Rambo?" I glanced in the living room. No JR. Hmm? He'd be around somewhere, I supposed. Calling him periodically as I diced the tomatoes and prepared the poblano peppers, I started to get a bit worried. True, he'd pee'd all over me, regularly, but I didn't really wish Lisa would trade him in for a proper dog, often.

So where was he?

"Rambo?" I called again, heading back to the living room. "Rambo?!"

Nothing. I raced upstairs, checked bedrooms, under beds, bathroom. No dog. *Christ!* Seriously worried now, I went back to the living room. No sign. Not a dog's hair.

"Flint?" I scratched my head. "Any ideas?"

In answer to which, Flint burped. I paled. Then almost passed out, as the bird imitated the washing machine on rickety fast-spin.

"Oh, *fu*... No." I felt the blood drain from my face. Galvanizing myself into action, I shot to the kitchen. *Jesus.* He hadn't, had he? Queasy to the pit of my stomach, I watched the drum spin round. Please God, don't let him...

The drum slowed.

Then clunked to a shuddery halt.

I swallowed, hard, and sweating, reached shakily for the door.

Hardly able to breathe past the lump in my throat, I peered inside, and...

Clothes sandwiched against the drum. But no dog. Thank God! My heart kicked in again. "Rambo?!!"

My mouth dry, I ran to the back garden. Had I opened the door? Must have. Oh, no, the frickin' back gate was open. *Jesus Christ*, Lisa loves that dog. I mean, like a baby. She'll kill me. I'll kill myself.

What was I going to do? Ring around the local dog pounds, check online for available oddly-spotted, piddly Jack Russells with attitude? No chance.

Falling over a patio chair, I flew toward the gate, then stopped, dead. There behind the mop bucket, so small I could easily have missed him, was a tiny, oddly spotted, Rottie/JR.

And he was trembling.

I gulped, thoroughly ashamed. Was it me he was scared of, or Flint? Careless of teeth and other bits best avoided, I hoisted the little fellow up, held him high, and laughed. Rambo was too boggle-eyed with surprise to pee.

"D'y'know, I think I can see what Lisa sees in you. Kinda cute, aren't you?" I lowered the dog down, figuring he needed a bit of reassurance and nestled him in my arms, then... Oh, what the heck... planted a kiss on top of his head.

"I think I could even learn to love you." I spoke softly in his pointy ear.

"Me too." Lisa said, blinking back a tear as she stared at me. "The, um, gate was open."

I'm not sure whether it was the *Chilli Peppers* or my declaration of love for Rambo that did it. Whatever, it worked. I pulled Lisa closer as, appetites satiated, we cuddled on the sofa.

Asked what she'd fancied for dessert, Lisa had fixed me with huge, nervous eyes, and blurted she quite fancied... the naked chef. She blushed so beautifully then, my heart melted.

"*Who's a clever boy then?*" Flint squawked, nutting his bell.

"Adam." Lisa smiled, stroking Rambo's tummy, as he lay on his back, legs akimbo, between us.

We swapped another spoonful of ice cream and were mopping the excess from each other's lips when the answering machine kicked in.

Mom, again. "Adam," she said. "Now, I know I was a bit rude about Lucy. I'm sure she's completely adorable..."

"Completely," I agreed, lingering over a drip.

"...and can't help being a little bit odd." Well done, Mom, I winced.

"Anyway, I just rang to remind you to remind Lucy about the golf club do she said she'd help me cater for. It would be a tremendous help with my being incapacitated, so if you could just let her know it's a week on Saturday. Nothing too ostentatious. I thought a choice of starters might be nice, three possibly? A choice of soup too, obviously, and mains and desserts, of course. A select would be nice, and one or two nibbles served with the coffee, perhaps? Tell Lucy to..."

Lisa choked.

"At least we know one of the starters will be a hit," I offered. "You'd have to up the ingredients, of course." I shrugged, hopefully. As in hoping this wasn't goodbye.

"*Ye-es.*" Lisa smiled, her eyes in blink overdrive and her voice rather high-pitched as she studied my menu.

"I'll just, um, give Becky a ring. Make sure she's, um..." Lisa scrambled back to the kitchen for her cell phone.

Chilli Peppers

Ingredients for 2 portions:

4 poblano peppers (if you cannot find those, bell peppers or any other 5-6 inch long mild pepper can be substituted)

1 pound of ground meat (whichever you prefer, half pork and half beef is best, but it really is up to you)

1 jalapeño (or another hot pepper; more if you like it hot)

1 shallot

1 garlic clove

4 plum tomatoes

½ cup of grated cheese (again, your preference: cheddar, mozzarella, gouda, ...)

Salt, freshly ground pepper

2 tsp olive oil

1 cup fresh mixed herbs (a combination of basil, tarragon, oregano, parsley, rosemary)

Cooking instructions:

Dice the shallot, cover in freshly ground pepper and put to the side.

Add one teaspoon olive oil to a pan and start the stove on medium heat. Peel the garlic and cut it into small pieces. You can use a garlic press if you prefer. Wash the jalapeño and carefully cut it into tiny pieces (with the seeds). Make sure you really wash your hands afterwards and do not rub your eyes (particularly if you actually want to be able to see what you eat). Add the garlic, meat, and jalapeño to the pan and slowly fry it until the meat is lightly browned and crumbly.

Pre-heat your oven to 350°F.

Now, dice the tomatoes and chop the washed herbs. Add to the meat once that's cooked all the way through. Season with salt and pepper.

Turn off the stove and take care of the peppers now: cut them in half lengthwise and remove the seeds. You can leave the stem on, it adds to the decorative effect (but you should not eat it later). Wash the peppers now so all the seeds are gone.

Place the pepper halves in an oven-proof dish greased with olive oil and fill them with the meat sauce. If there is more meat sauce than fits in the pepper halves, distribute this around them. Bake the peppers for 15 minutes. Place them on plates and serve hot, sprinkled with the shallot and cheese. You can serve fresh bread as a side to mop up any remaining sauce.

Chapter 3 Menu Fit for a Queen

"Here you go." Becky passed me the menu she'd been sweating over half the night. "Let's see Her Maj find fault with that."

"Thanks, Becks, you're a star." I stopped contemplating gnawing on the edge of the table in favor of my newly-gelled nails, took another huge slug of wine while I perused — then choked, again.

"You have to be joking," I spluttered, as Becky skidded around the table to give me a hearty slap on the back. "I can't cook that! I can't cook!"

"'Course you can. You've only got to cook a third of it, anyway. And I'll be with you every step of the way."

"How?! And how?! And will you *please* stop doing that?"

"*Sorr-ee*, I am sure." Becky ceased in her rather too hearty ministrations to my back. "I was only trying to help."

"I know you were." I sighed, contrite. Poor Becky had worked so hard, putting together a menu that might meet with royal approval, i.e. Adam's mother's, and I was being totally ungrateful. "You *are*, but... how?" I repeated, blinking forlornly at her list, which, in my capable hands, might well turn out to be a weapon of mass destruction.

"Multitasking," Becky informed me matter-of-factly, swiping up the wine bottle as she went back to her chair.

"*Ahh.*" I heaved out another sigh, and, none the wiser, scraped my chair back to feed Rambo, who was gazing wanly at naught but his reflection in the bottom of his steel doggy dish. "I feel so much more enlightened now," I told her, a touch facetiously, as I spooned home-cooked boiled chicken into the dish.

"You might want to enlighten Rambo then." Becky helped herself to a handful of Pringles, which were the only select nibbles to be had in this house, and nodded at Rambo, who was gamely trying to tackle the contents of the wine glass I'd placed in front of him, ably demonstrating my obviously missing multitasking gene.

"Flip." I skidded back over with his dish. "No, sweetie," I said, attempting to remove the glass, before Rambo's alcohol content exceeded his miniature JR body mass. "Not that, babe. It's Mommy's."

"*Grrrrrr.*" Rambo apparently disagreed.

"Rambo, leave!" I commanded, asserting my alpha authority. "It's Mommy's!"

Instantly obedient — not — Rambo blithely continued lapping at his beverage.

Humph. I whipped the glass from under his nose and plonked the dish in its place.

Communicating his thoughts on my questionable culinary skills, Rambo sniffed at the contents, curled a lip I would swear, then stumpy-tail flat against rump, waddled to the cat flap and out of the back door.

Doomed, I thought, blinking down at my rebuffed rubbery offering. The whole thing was doomed to spectacular failure. "You were saying?" I wandered slumpy-shouldered back over to Becky.

"Multitasking," Becky repeated, and helped herself to more wine. "And hands-free."

"Pardon?" Sounded like a recipe for disaster to me.

Becky obviously noticed my befuddled look. "*I'll* be doing the multitasking," she expounded. "*You'll* be doing the hands-free."

"Right." I nodded, brow knitted. "Nope, sorry, don't get it."

"Oh, for goodness sake, Lisa, it's not rocket science."

"It is," I assured her.

"Look..." she dragged her chair to my side of the table and smoothed out her menu, entitled '*The Plan*' "...it's quite easy to follow. I've number-coded everything, see? You're number one, because you are. Adam's six, because he's hot, especially in a teensy-weensy hand-towel... sigh... and I'm two, because I will be there too.

The Plan

Starters:

1: Faith in Salad (a couscous, chicken and grape salad seemingly directly from Heaven, great in summer)

6: Chilli Peppers (red pepper halves, filled with Chilli Con Carne; a twist on the traditional Texan dish)

2: Cheese Cream Ahoi (Bavarian Cheese Cream)

Soups:

1: Green Soup (cold, green Gazpacho)

2: Red Soup (red beet soup Borschtsch style)

6: White Soup (white asparagus cream soup)

Mains:

1: Drunken Chicken (chicken in wine with green beans)

6: Olivia's Pride (vegetarian spinach lasagna, named after Popeye's girlfriend Olivia)

2: Poseidon Serves Up (baked fish with seasonal vegetables)

Desserts:

1: Frisian Anchor (red berry compote)

6: Zebra (chocolate pudding with yogurt)

2: Peach Gobbler (peach cobbler, to gobble down)

Coffee Time:

2: Cassata Seduction (an Italian cake-curd concoction)

1: Pizza Cookie (a huge cookie, baked on a pizza sheet)

6: Chockfull of Zucchinis (chocolate zucchini cake, great when you have too many zucchinis in your garden and nobody wants to see another glass of pickled zucches)

Select:

6: Stack O'Cakes (American-style stack of pancakes)

2: Jammed in There (jam)

2: Impress the In-Laws (avocado fudge)

29

"See," Becky beamed, "not complicated at all." I blanched, white. "Rambo," I called weakly, in need of the comfort of a little soft body next to my own, the chances of a red-hot body next to mine ever again being nil after I'd wiped out the entire membership of the golf club, including Her Maj, the she-witch mother.

Rambo rattled through the cat flap, a soggy, furry rat — fortunately the stuffed toy variety — in his mouth, rather than a dead fish-head, and completely ignored me.

"You've already made the *Faith in Salad* dish, so that one will be a doddle."

"Absolutely," I agreed pseudo-enthusiastically, and had a quick swig from the bottle.

"And Adam's *Chilli Peppers* were obviously a resounding success, *weren't* they?" Becky waggled her eyebrows suggestively.

I went from blanch to blush in a flash, though I probably did pass through green, feeling ever-so-slightly nauseous, as I was.

Becky gave me a nudge. "Come on then, share," she said, giving me another conspiratorial nudge — I did wish she'd desist, before I fell off the chair. "Is he as hot in bed as he is naked?"

"Do you mind?" I said grimly. "He was *not* naked."

"No," Becky tittered, "he was leaving a little bit to the imagination." She paused to ponder, a smirk tugging at her flawlessly-glossed lips. Honestly, did she have to be a master-chef extraordinaire *and* perfect in every department?

"Ahem," I interrupted her musings. "He was, *actually*," I informed her, glancing nonchalantly at my only flawless bit, my gelled nails.

Becky's eyes shot wide. "OhmiGod, you've hit the jackpot!" she exclaimed, looking astonished, which left me a bit peeved. "Come on, let's get this done, hon. Show Her Maj what you're made of." She turned her attention decisively to *The Plan*.

"If I must." For Becky's sake, I tried, though the only clear-cut decision to me seemed to be suicide. "But why..."

"Why? *Why?*" Becky cut in, staring at me incredulously now. "Because you've only gone and bagged one, haven't you? A lesser-spotted, eligible, perfect man," she elaborated when I crinkled my much furrowed brow, clueless.

Becky hoisted up her shoulders, back ramrod-straight and definitely in *I-mean-business* mode.

"I have?"

Becky deflated a bit. "Honestly, Lisa…" She shook her head despairingly. "Yes!" She stated emphatically. "Okay, so he's probably not one-hundred percent perfect, but he's as close as dammit. And now you've bagged him, you have to ease Her Maj out the picture, fluff up your tail feathers and make sure you keep him."

"He's already got a bird," I informed her flatly. "A parrot. His name's Flint, and Adam loves him, bald spots and all."

"Perfect. One-hundred percent." Becky sighed, blinky-eyed. "Right, pay attention. We're going to do this, if it kills us."

"It very probably will," I muttered.

Becky gave me a look. "Do you want to have his babies or not?"

That's the thing about Becky. She can always be relied upon to get right to the point, embarrassingly. "Yes," I admitted, flushing down to my freckly décolleté, "but" — I gave her a look this time, which hopefully read *interrupt me at your own peril* — "why do I have to get Adam involved in the cooking?"

"Because he *can* cook!" Becky rolled her eyes so high, her eyebrows disappeared. "And it is his moth…"

"But that's the problem," I wailed. "So can his mother. So could his wife."

"Oh, Lisa, Lisa, whatever happened to your confidence?" Becky emitted another soulful sigh. "Don't answer that," she added quickly.

I didn't need to. Becky was there when it took off after my ex took up with the slim, young thing with breasts implants and panache in the kitchen.

We paused to regroup, Rambo goose-stepping purposefully back in as we did. Oh, Rambo with his spotty little paws. Almost as if he knew I needed a little reassurance, he headed for his dish, plucked up a bit of indigestible chicken and — headed for the cat flap.

"So, tell him then," Becky suggested, at length. "Let yourself off the hook, and just tell Adam you can't cook. There's nothing else for it. You're going to have to come clean, Lisa. It's either that or get through the mother test, and then get yourself on a cookery course, fast. Though why you should try to change yourself for a man…. What I'm trying to say is, he should love you, bald spots, flaws and all."

Thank you. That's bolstered the old self-esteem no end. The shoulders went into permanent decline.

"And if he doesn't, he's not worth…"

"She was beautiful," I blurted. "His wife, she was… beautiful."

I glanced at Becky with a mixture of hopelessness and shame. I wasn't jealous of the obviously perfect woman who'd been Adam's wife. Adam had given me no cause to be. But when the gloss wore off in approximately 48 hours, as it was bound to at the golf club do, then he would have cause to bid me be a not-so-fond *au revoir*.

Best friend in the whole world though she was, I didn't really expect Becky to understand. She was so stunning, men fell at her feet. Not that Becky walked all over them, but she'd certainly never been dumped or cheated on.

"You mean..." Becky gawped, "...he has photos?!"

"They were married, Becky," I pointed out. "He's bound to have."

"Yes, but... around? I mean, while you and he...?"

"No!" I immediately jumped to Adam's defense. He was quite entitled to have photos around. You can't just obliterate memories, nor would I expect him to. The fact is, though, one of the many qualities that endeared him to me — apart from his towel and the fact that he obviously adored Rambo — was that he'd been thoughtful enough not to leave them on display. "He'd taken them down," I went on, less stridently. "He's that sort. Thoughtful."

"Oh, right." Seemingly satisfied, Becky climbed off her high horse.

"I couldn't help but notice them though," I continued, "when I was nosing through his CD collection."

"As one does." Becky nodded and topped up our glasses.

"Adam shouted from the kitchen for me to select what I fancied and put one on. I was searching for the CD control — and there were the framed photos, all neatly stacked in a drawer. And, um, well, his housework skills are obviously not on a par with his cooking, if the tell-tale impressions in the dust on the shelf were anything to judge by."

"One-hundred-and-one percent." Becky sniffled, took a tissue from her bag and dabbed daintily.

"She really was very pretty."

Becky reached for my hand. "And you feel inadequate?"

"Uh-huh." I dragged half a toilet paper roll from up my sleeve and blew noisily. "Because of my own insecurities, I suppose."

We both had another sniffle and a sip of wine in contemplative silence.

My heavy heart was buoyed a little though, as Rambo shot through the cat flap for his third, successive chunk of chicken.

"Sweetie," Becky said eventually, "his wife's gone. And from what you've said, he obviously cares about you. You don't have to compete in his mind, I'd bet a month's salary on it. His mom's, probably…"

"Exactly." I partook of a huge wallop of wine. "I can't let him down, Becky. I've already said I would do it. And even if his mom is a complete cow, she has just had her op, and… Oh, God, what am I going to do."

"Multitasking," Becky reiterated forcefully. "And hands-free. It's just cooking, Lisa," she went on, as — no doubt looking mystified — I contemplated how one cooked with no hands. "And at least Rambo's having a bash at his food now. Proof of the pudding and all that."

"Yes." I smiled, watching Rambo strut past with yet another lump of gourmet doggy food, a little trail of mud in his wake, I noticed. "Rambo?" I stopped him short of the cat flap.

Rambo glanced back at me over a mud-encrusted snout, sneezed, wagged his stump, flicked the flap and zipped on out.

"Proof of the pudding," I offered, as Becky and I gazed at the molehill that had appeared on the lawn.

"Aw, look at his perked-up little ears," Becky said, gazing at his perked-up bottom, as Rambo worked fervently at his endeavors. "He's burying it in case he's hungry later."

"No, Becks." I sighed, a fresh bout of foreboding as to the fate of the members of the golf club washing over me. "He's burying it because he's hungry now. Rambo, come on, hon. Chum!"

"Um, I'll do two of the dishes in advance, I think." Becky mused as my traitorous dog abandoned his molehill and skidded delightedly in. "That'll free me up to help out more on the day."

I love Lisa, I really do. I could even forgive her cooking, as long as I didn't end up doing it.

Normally, I wouldn't mind, but trying to work out how to tell one's supposed-to-be fiancé you'd rather he moved out than marry him, makes for trying times. He's in bed now. Still, at midday. Jobless, still, and sulking after throwing a hissy fit because I'd switched on the lamp early this morning in order to facilitate seeing, which was 'selfish and thoughtless and treating him as if he didn't exist', apparently. Fleetingly, I'd wondered whether to sit on the pillow when he stuffed his head under it, but I'd really rather the alien was out of my house than dead in my bed. Who was this man I'd allowed to invade my life? This person, who, instead of holding me in a consoling embrace when my beloved Bagpuss went missing, went out?

We'd had loads in common when we'd met, or so I thought. Both loved cooking and travelling. Had the same sense of humor. The relationship quickly became serious. And when it did, Ryan decided he wasn't ready for commitment.

He'd been scared of trusting again, he'd said when he'd rung for the millionth time after we'd split and I'd finally picked up. He loved me, missed me; wanted to marry me. He was sorry. He needed me. What he needed, it turned out, was somewhere to live, preferably somewhere with a spare room where he could accommodate his two children alternate weekends.

The spare room has now been converted to a children's bedroom, complete with PCs and PlayStations. The children he deposits there and then promptly abandons so he can offer his emotional support to his rugby team.

As for the cooking, he barely looks up from the TV when I come home from work. The thrill of the chase has obviously worn off — and my patience has worn thin.

Banishing the *boy*friend from hell from my mind on the basis that Lisa would be there for me if I needed her, as she always had been, I ignored the snoring from the bedroom and concentrated on the soup. Lisa and I had hit the shops first thing, so at least all the ingredients were bought. Please God make that they all got divided out properly between us and at least one of us ended up with an intact relationship.

Red Soup

Ingredients for 4 portions:

2 garlic cloves

2 chilli peppers

2 red onions

2 cups red beets (cooked)

2 cups vegetable broth

2 tbsp olive oil

Salt, pepper

2 tbsp crème fraîche

Cooking instructions:

If you buy the red beets cooked in a glass, make sure there is no added sugar. That way, you can even use the juice the beets come in and substitute that for some of the broth. The color result will be even more stunning.

If you buy fresh beets, dice them first (make sure you are wearing gloves and a pinny, unless you want red hands and naturally-dyed jeans). Cook them (the beets, not your jeans) barely covered in water for 10-15 minutes. Again, you can keep the water and substitute it for some of the broth. Reserve some of the dice for decoration.

Add all ingredients except for the crème fraîche and the beets held back for decoration into a blender and puree them. You may have to do this in two batches; that's alright – you can combine them again later.

Pour the soup into soup bowls, decorate with a dollop of crème fraîche and some diced beet.

You can serve this soup hot or cold.

There. Job done. Obviously, I'd have to add the decoration when it was served, and I'd had to up the ingredients to cater for more than four, but as recipe goes, easy as pie.

Humming happily, I headed to the bathroom for a quick freshen up and ran into Ryan, scratching his armpit and yawning as he came out.

Oh, he'd left me a present. How thoughtful. Stubble in the sink and discarded clothes on the floor. Enough was enough.

"Ryan," I said calmly, following him to the kitchen, "do you think you could leave the bathroom as you find it please, i.e. clean?"

"And do you think you could ever stop criticizing?" He turned on me, looking at me definitely not in the way lovers do. "Maybe then you could find time to produce some food around here that isn't to be consumed by someone else?"

Alternatively, with so much time on your hands maybe *you* could, I refrained from saying for fear of provoking further argument. And then felt my blood boil for myself and all people in a relationship who lived in fear of doing or saying the wrong thing. For Lisa, whose previous partner had left her confidence in tatters.

"A man could die of starvation around here. It's a wonder my kids don't go home emaciated." He looked me derisorily up and down and turned to the fridge.

"You poor thing," I murmured. "You do look a bit pale, now you come to mention it. Never mind, a good hearty helping of soup will soon fix that."

"Oh, right, thanks. I didn't think you cared." Ryan turned back, his look one of pleasant surprise.

Followed by out-and-out shock. *Sppplottch!*

"There, you're a much better color now." I flicked a stunning red drip from my fingers onto his startled and equally stunning red face. "Goodbye, Ryan. The door is *that* way. I'm sure you can manage to find that all on your own, unlike the stove, washing machine, vacuum. Oh, and just in case you can't, Lisa and her boyfriend are on their way over. He's a policeman. A rather muscular one. I'm sure he'll be happy to assist you."

That was a big fat fib, of course. Lisa and her boyfriend were probably up to their eyeballs in their respective ingredients by now, but hey, any port in a storm.

"Tum-ti-tum." I had another little hum to myself as Ryan dripped out of the front door, belongings-too-big-to-carry to follow. Good thing my *Red Soup* recipe *is* a quick and easy one.

Chapter 4 Anything for Love

The *Cassata Seduction* (an Italian cake-curd concoction), I'd made last week for poor, starving rat-bag Ryan's birthday, had been simply delicious. His emaciated, neglected by *moi* — huh! — children had scoffed at least half of it, wiping their sticky chocolate fingers on my scrimped and saved-for sofa in the process. That being a tried-and-tested hit then, I'd included it on Lisa's menu and prepared another cake, which was now ready to fill, before coating in apricot jam and oodles of melted chocolate tomorrow. *Yummy.*

Having sliced the cake into four lengthwise, I was just spreading the layers with the filling — a finger-licking combination of butter, curd cheese, sweet-cream, sugar, vanilla extract, orange liquor, candied fruits, baking chocolate and candied ginger — when there was a frantic hammering at the front door.

Downing tools, I dashed to answer, thinking it must be an emergency, to find my seventy-five-year old neighbor, Madge Meadows, wiltily clutching the doorframe. "Madge?" Lord, she looked peaky. "What on earth's wrong? Come on, come on in." I eased an arm around her shoulders. "Can I get you something? Tea? Water?"

Looking a bit desperate now, a hand to her chest, Madge finally managed to croak, "A man..."

I arched an eyebrow. "Beg pardon?"

"...out there." She waved a hand urgently toward the lift area. "He's covered in blood!" she cried, wide-eyed. "It's awful; all over his clothes! We have to call an..."

I rolled my eyes. "It's not." I sighed.

Madge blinked, confused.

"It's not a man, Madge. It's Ryan."

Madge straightened up. "Your boyfriend?"

"Ex," I clarified.

"The one who went off to play tennis when your poor Bagpuss went missing?"

"That's the one." I shrugged sadly.

"Oh, well, that's all right then." Madge bustled on in. "Mmm, something smells scrumptious," she commented, dying Ryan forgotten as she sniffed the air on the way to the kitchen.

"*Cassata Seduction.*" I closed the door as the man himself appeared on the landing, looking sorry for himself and still wearing his red-soup-assaulted shirt.

"For Lisa's golf club do," I called after Madge. "She's catering."

Ryan rang the doorbell.

I headed for the kitchen.

"You mean *you're* catering." Madge chuckled. "You're a good girl, Becky. I wish I had friends like... Ooh, my," she came to a halt at the cooling rack, "that does look delicious. Makes me feel quite peckish."

"Would you like a slice with your tea?" I took the hint.

"Oh, no, I couldn't possibly." Madge eyed the cake longingly. "I'm watching my waistline. You never know when Mr. Right might come along, do you?"

"Shame. I have one I prepared earlier." I hid a smile as I fetched the leftovers of the previous cake from the fridge and unveiled it. Madge was determined to find Mr. Right before she threw in the towel. Though what she'd do with him if she did? The washer repairman had made a hasty exit from her apartment the other day, looking a bit panicky, I'd noticed.

"Oh, well, if you need help eating it up." Madge parked herself at the table in one second flat. "Men are overrated anyway. Chocolate's better than sex any day."

"My thoughts entirely." Smirking, I passed her a slice and fork and ignored Mr. Wrong who'd obviously let himself in with his key and was standing in the kitchen doorway, now looking bemused, as well as abused.

"I need to get some clothes," he said, with a woeful little sigh.

I poured the tea.

"Thought it better I didn't walk around naked as well as homeless," Ryan went on.

"Oooh, orgasm-inducing." Madge closed her eyes in ecstasy as she munched on a mouthful of *Cassata Seduction*.

Ryan curled a lip, confused. "Flattered, I'm sure."

"Would you like another slice?" I asked Madge. "There's plenty now there's only me here." I shot Ryan a pointed glance.

"Well... go on then, if you insist." Madge said, around another mouthful. "It really is delicious. You should take this up professionally, you know, Becky."

"Right, well," Ryan fidgeted in the doorway, "I'll just go and get some clothes and a few of my things, then."

"Give up that job at the hospital and run a little catering company."

"Nice idea, Madge." I sighed wistfully. I adored cooking. For me it was never a chore, more a creative outlet. One stifled by Ryan, I now realized. "A pipe dream though, unfortunately."

"And then I'll go." Ryan continued wretchedly.

"I'd have to find premises," I addressed Madge.

"Forever," Ryan added solemnly.

"And before I did that, I'd have to build up a client list. And what with working full time..."

"Fade away into oblivion." Ryan paused, and waited. "Possibly never to be seen again."

Oscar material, definitely. I passed Madge her cup. "I mean. I'd love to give running my own business a go, but there just aren't enough hours in the day, Madge."

"Well you'll have more time on your hands now that useless boyfriend has gone," Madge suggested, wiping her finger around her plate and then licking off the chocolate.

"Ahem!" Ryan coughed. "I'm not sure *where* I'll go, of course."

"And you don't need premises." Madge helped herself to the last slice of cake. "You could set up a website and Facebook page and connect with people on Twatter."

"Twitter, Madge." I laughed, though uber-impressed by how computer-savvy she seemed to be compared to me.

"Yes, but I'd have to pay a website designer," I told her, anything more than typing up menus was beyond me. "And to do that I'd have to get all the recipes photographed beforehand. It's a nice idea, but..."

Ryan sighed. "Don't mind me," he said, a tad impatiently.

"But nothing..." Madge tutted. "You can always find excuses if you look hard enough, Becky. My nephew, Luke, could do your website design."

Ryan sighed again, demonstratively. "I'll just collect my paltry belongings then, shall I, and then find a doorstep to sleep on?"

"Right. Fine. Thank you for your concern." He waited again, then turned to slope dejectedly up the hall when it was clear nobody was the least bit concerned at all.

"He's a lovely boy," Madge expounded. "His website designs are terribly good. He did the Waitrose campaign, did you know? Took all the photos. He's extremely talented. And..." Madge paused for a quick lick of her plate "...he's also extremely handsome."

Ryan's head reappeared around the doorframe. "Who is?"

"But I can't afford him, Madge."

"Nonsense." Madge speared the last crumb from the serving plate. "Like I say, he's a lovely boy, not like that ungrateful *ex*-boyfriend of yours. He'd do it for you at cut-price, I'm sure. In fact," she had a little think, "he has his mom's birthday bash coming up soon. A biggie, so... you scratch his back, my lovely, and I'm quite sure he'll scratch yours."

Ryan's whole body twanged back into view. "Oh, no, he frickin' won't," he said, his cheeks flushed as red as his soup-stained shirt. "If there's any back-scratching to be done around here, *I'll* be doing it."

In your dreams, dude. Ignoring Ryan, I paused to ponder. "Luke isn't the one with the dark-hair, is he, and the gorgeous, er..." I waved a hand about my body, envisaging Luke's, which looked hot and honed in all the rights places under a white tee and jeans when I'd glanced briefly at him — for the five minutes or so he'd ambled on the forecourt taking a phone call.

"Suntan?" Madge supplied. "All over, my dear," she assured me, with a lewd wink. "He's naturally dark and swarthy. *And* single."

"Becky, this has gone far enough." Ryan obviously decided to assert himself.

"Shove off, loser!" Madge decided to do likewise.

"And leave your key when you do." I giggled, as Ryan blinked, startled, then turned uncertainly back up the hall.

"Right, I'd better get off," Madge said, easing herself from her chair. "That was lovely, dear, thank you. *Will you be all right?*" she mouthed.

"Perfectly," I assured her, as Ryan sloped past again with an overnight bag.

"Well, you know where I am if you need me. Luke's also a black belt in Origami," she shouted, for Ryan's benefit, no doubt. "He's popping over to see me in five minutes, coincidentally. Such a caring boy."

Aikido, I assumed she meant, stifling a laugh as Ryan passed the door again, a bit quicker of step this time, a wary look on his face and clutching his laptop.

"You just shout, my dear, if you have any trouble." Madge gave me a reassuring pat on the hand. "Luke's flying kick to the crotch has bullies thinking twice, mark my words."

Ryan winced as he passed by the door again, then returned sharpish — with his potted plant.

"Ooh, I've just thought," Madge paused in the hall, "I said I'd do the cake for the birthday bash, but yours tastes far better than anything I could make."

"Oh, well, I don't mind baking you one, Madge," I offered, thinking of her arthritic hands. "If you let me know when it…"

"No, no, I wouldn't dream of taking advantage, dear." Madge held up a silencing hand. "Unlike some people." She scowled pointedly at Ryan, who, under scrutiny, swiftly removed his key from his key ring.

"But I'd love the recipe." Madge smiled sweetly back at me.

"Here you go. It is the most difficult recipe in my book, but simply delicious."

Madge and I perused the recipe together, as Ryan took his leave, assuring us we needn't trouble ourselves about him being found malnourished and suffering from hypothermia on the canal embankment.

"We won't," I assured him. "Don't forget to close the door on the way out."

Cassata Seduction

Total preparation and waiting time 2-3 days! Ingredients for one Cassata (8-10 slices).

For the cake:

5 tbsp hot water

½ cup sugar

marrow from 1 vanilla bean (stick the scraped bean into your sugar pot for some scrumtuous vanilla sugar or into the container you keep your ground coffee in for some naturally-flavored vanilla coffee!)

½ cup all-purpose flour

3 eggs

½ cup starch (corn starch or potato starch will work)

3 tsp baking powder

Oil or grease for the cake form

some flour for the form

For the filling:

½ cup and 1 tbsp butter

2 cups cream curd cheese (can be substituted with ricotta cheese)

2 tbsp sweet cream

2 tbsp sugar

marrow from 1 vanilla bean

4 tsp orange liquor

1 cup candied or dried fruits (mixed, depending on preference), cut small

3 tbsp candied or dried ginger, cut small

2 cups baking chocolate, cut small

For the glazing:

1 cup apricot jam

2 cups dark chocolate (or white, if you prefer)

2 tbsp butter

To make the cake:

Pre-heat your oven to 175°C.

Grease a 27-cm bread-shaped cake form and swirl some flour around the form, covering the entire inside. This will enable you to get the cake out of the form without damaging it later.

Separate the egg white from the egg yolks. Beat the egg whites until stiff. In a large bowl, combine the egg yolks, water, sugar and vanilla and beat until creamy.

In a medium bowl, mix together the flour, starch and baking powder. Add the stiff egg whites to the egg yolk mixture, sift the flour mixture over top and fold together with a silicone spatula or an egg beater.

Pour the dough into the prepared form. Bake at 175°C for about 45 minutes. When the cake is done, turn out onto a cooling rack and let cool completely (24 hours is best).

To make the filling:

Beat the butter until creamy. Press the whey out of the cream curd cheese. Mix the curd, sweet cream, sugar, vanilla bean marrow and the orange liquor together. When homogenous, add the (candied) fruits, baking chocolate and (candied) ginger to the mixture.

Wash the cake form and line it with aluminum foil, making sure the foil comes over the edges. This will help taking the cake out once it is set.

Cut the cake lengthwise into four layers. Place the bottom layer back into the cake form and spread one third of the filling over this layer. Add the next layer, press together gently and spread the next third of the filling over top. Add the third layer, press together gently and spread the last third of the filling over top. Place the last layer (top of the cake) on top of this and press together gently. Cover the cake with aluminum foil, sealing it as tightly as possible to the cake form, so that no filling can escape. Place a bread board or a flat board on top of the cake and weigh it down to keep pressure on the whole cake. Cool the cake over night in the refrigerator or a very cool, dark room.

On the next day, turn out the cake onto a cake rack or wide cake serving plate. If you are using a cake rack, place aluminum foil under the rack.

Press the apricot jam through a sieve and heat in a small saucepan, stirring constantly, but do not boil. When heated, spread the jam evenly over the entire cake. Let the jam cool and dry completely for at least two hours.

Melt the chocolate with the butter and spread evenly over the entire cake. Let the cake cool entirely in the refrigerator for at least two more hours before serving it.

To cut the cake, use a heated, serrated knife.

A round cake form can be used to achieve a more gateau-type Cassata Seduction. The chocolate glaze can be white, milk, or dark chocolate, depending on your preference, or you could glaze half the cake white and the other dark to please everybody. The outside of the cake can be decorated with dried or candied fruit or marzipan figures and ribbons.

I'd just struggled up the hall with the entire supermarket stock, when my cell phone rang for the third time.

Mom, again, I supposed. "Yes?" I answered shortly, dumping bags and groping my phone from my pocket. "Oh hi, Becky." I clutched the phone to my ear as Flint carried on imitating my ringtone merrily in the background. "Yep, got the lot," I assured her, pleased with my recipe shopping efforts, despite a finicky moment with the zucchini. The sales assistant hadn't been overly impressed when I'd asked her if size mattered.

"Everything, yes," I assured Becky, quoting my list and reeling off a bazillion ingredients with which to cook *Chilli Peppers*, which had obviously been a bit of a hit — I smiled quietly, *White Asparagus Cream Soup*, *Olivia's Pride* — a vegetarian spinach lasagne named after Popeye's girlfriend named Olivia in German, so Becky had said. There was also something aptly named *Zebra*, a chocolate pudding with yogurt, served in a cocktail glass, layered to look like a zebra and served with a cookie. She'd been at pains to point this out — obviously enthusiastic about her menu. I could see why: they were definitely original. Then there was *Chockfull of Zucchinis*, a chocolate zucchini cake, which actually might have been not quite so chock-full had the sales assistant not come grudgingly to my rescue... but chocolate and zucchini together in a cake? That threw me, I have to admit; but then, I'm no cook.

Lastly, *Stack O'Cakes*, a stack of pancakes American style. Easy as pie, apparently. To some, possibly, but I was frickin' glad I wasn't cooking any of it. And if Lisa producing this little lot, along with several other dishes, didn't earn due approval, I'd be divorcing my mother, no question.

"So where do you want it?" I asked Becky, checking through the bags to make sure I had got everything, including enough Oreo cookies (I hadn't been able to resist snatching a few, they were so irresistible).

"What do you mean, where do I want it?" Beck sounded a bit puzzled.

"The food," I clarified, as Flint went into Boeing-747-flying-overhead mode. "Where do you want... Flint! Zip it or eBay!

"Sorry, parrot's got a death wish." I turned back to the phone. "I swear one of these days I'll have him stuffed and mounted."

Becky didn't reply.

"Erm, I am joking, Becky," I assured her. "I don't habitually go around stuffing and mounting birds."

"Glad to hear it," Becky retorted dryly.

Uh, oh. She was obviously an animal lover and obviously not amused.

"Often," I tried.

Silence.

"Ahem. So, where do you want the…"

"Adam," Becky cut in, "I realize you have a sense of humor, and I'm glad for Lisa that you do. God knows she could do with the smile putting back on her face, but could you please stop now before I'm forced to kill you."

I glanced at my phone. Bit drastic, wasn't it? I mean, I knew my jokes were bad, but…

"In your oven, Adam," Becky cut through my deliberations, "is where I want the food. Prepare what you can tonight, the *Chilli Peppers*, I imagine can be pre-prepared; then cook the rest tomorrow."

What?!! I stared, stunned now, at the phone. She was kidding. Wasn't she? Yes, she was. My heart slowed to a regular beat. Nice one, Becky. *Touché.*

"Lisa will be cooking her *Faith in Salad* and the *Green Soup* at home and taking them to the golf club around seven. We need to be there at precisely ten past," Becky went on seriously, scarily. These were most definitely not the headings on my recipe lists. "Lisa will meet us at the back door leading to the kitchen. The *Drunken Chicken, Frisian Anchor* and *Pizza Cookie*, she'll do in situ, so Her Maj… your mother …doesn't cotton on she hasn't done the lot. *Comprendre?*"

Christalmighty! My blood froze. She wasn't joking.

Crap.

"Adam? Adam, are you still there?"

No, I was having a beam-me-up moment. Raking hand shakily through my hair, I turned full circle amidst the chaos where once was a kitchen floor, and fervently wished I was anywhere but.

"Uh-huh," I croaked weakly.

"Lisa did tell you, didn't she?"

"Erm, she, um…" Frantically, I cast my mind back, trying to recall, because there was no way, absolutely no way, I would have agreed… to cook? This lot? Lisa wouldn't stand a snowball in hell's chance of pulling this off with my inept input. I realized that all hope of getting out was sinking fast. Lisa had asked me what I thought of *The Plan*.

"Complicated," I'd said. "But fabulous, if you can do it? Mom will be well-impressed. She'll probably have your name engraved on a plaque above the Lady Chairman of the Golf Club."

Lisa's kissable mouth had curved into a delighted smile. "It is a bit complicated though, isn't it?" she'd said, a worried little 'V' knitting her brow as my lips strayed toward hers. "I was, um, wondering if you'd mind helping out?" she asked hesitantly. "I know it's a bit of a cheat but I'm sure they sell everything in Tescos, so..."

I'd given in to temptation about then. How could I not when she'd fixed me with those huge, intoxicating eyes?

Shopping. I squeezed my own eyes shut. I'd thought she'd meant shopping.

And Lisa thought I could cook. And now I was screwed, totally. This was it, the end of a beautiful relationship that nearly was; unless by some miracle *I* could pull it off.

"Yes, yes, she did," I told Becky, pulling in a breath and praying hard for inspiration. Divine intervention. Anything. Because there was no way I was going to lose Lisa because of my frickin' meddling mother.

Lisa was the first girl I'd met who made me smile, properly, on the inside. I liked her. My heart did a peculiar little flip in my chest. I liked her a lot.

I decided I had to tell her: that I couldn't cook, that I was full of bullshit and lies, and that I'd let my mother bully her into this, which was unforgivable. Come clean and hope that Lisa could forgive me, and, God willing, still like me a little?

Not tonight though.

Tonight I had other important things to do. "Okay, Becky, gotta go." I steeled myself and reached for my naked-lady pinny. "Sorry about the jokes. Bad taste, if you'll forgive the pun. Thanks for the heads up. I'll meet you out back of the golf club at 19:10 hours precisely."

Becky blew out a sigh of relief. "Thanks, Adam," she said. "You're an angel. Happy cooking!"

An angel, I very much doubted I was. Dead I might well be after this. I picked up the ingredients list, attached to which were recipes that would make Gary Rhodes' hair stand on end.

"Happy cooking? She really does have to be joking," I muttered, heading back to the hall for the last of the bags.

"*Squaawk.*" Flint nutted his bell. "*Happy cook...*"

"Yeah, yeah, hilarious Flint. Not." "*Caw, caw.*"

Chapter 5 Saturday Morning Fever

"Yes, sweetie, Mommy *has* got a Rambo bag!" I assured my eager little JR as, a million ingredients strewn about the kitchen, I finally revealed the Pets At Home bag I'd been hiding. I know I spoil him, but a reward for Mommy being otherwise engaged — having a nervous breakdown at the thought of catering for the golf club do — I thought was justified on this occasion.

In any case, "I love you, don't I, baby, hmm?"

"*Rrrowf, rrrowf. Yeah, yeah, hurry up,*" went Rambo, stump wagging frenziedly, little front legs bouncing excitedly.

"*Grrrowf, grrrowf.*" He panted round full-circle, then — boing — sprang up and stuffed his snout in the bag.

"*Snuffle. Snuffle.*" Tug. "*Grrrrr.*"

"All right. All right! Mommy's getting it!" I laughed as, hind legs on tippy-toe, he ferreted frantically around for his present.

"Rambo, down!" I instructed, now in serious-mistress mode. Plastic bags and doggy snouts were not a good combination.

"*Grrrrrowf, Grrrrr.*" Instantly obedient, Rambo ripped off a bit of plastic and had a quick chomp on it before spitting it out. Then he went boggled-eyed with delight, as I presented him with a huge, pink pig, embedded with no less than *three* tantalizing squeakies. "*Rrrowf, rowwwf.*" Wag, wag.

Being intelligent as well as a ferocious, fanged rat-catcher Rambo needs toys that are both indestructible and do something other than lie meekly down and die.

That one was definitely going to fight back, I decided, as Rambo gave Piggy a neck-breaking good shake, before strutting off, head high — necessarily, the pig being bigger than he was — to his bed to embark on a squeaking frenzy.

Right, onward. I puffed up my fringe, drew in a breath, contemplated swigging back a bottle of wine and retiring to bed. Then I remembered I'd quite prefer my gorgeous new man, Adam, in it — in order to achieve which, I had to metamorphose into Delia and win his mom over — and went bravely back to the fray instead.

The *Faith in Salad* hadn't been a doddle exactly, especially for someone who sometimes struggles with opening boxes, but it had definitely been easier second time around. I'd gone for organic chicken breasts for quickness this time, which made for a happier cook, even if the chicken wasn't over the moon.

The grape-based salad and curry chutney dressing I'd already prepared, boxed up and refrigerated, along with the rice. I had thought about doing the rice fresh at the golf club, but given I'd be wrestling with *Drunken Chicken, Frisian Anchor, Pizza Cookie* and well on my way to a heart attack, I'd decided against it. Miraculously, with the menu timings being spot on it hadn't congealed into a gooey mess. Phew.

Okay, so, next on the list: *Green Soup*, also to be served cold, ergo easily prepared beforehand, hopefully. If only all the recipes were, then I could deposit the food, wipe any incriminating fingerprints from the dishes, and scarper before the murder squad arrived.

Soup! I concentrated on the ingredients, rather than what my future might be like without Adam, now that I'd fallen a little bit, madly, deeply, truly in love with the man. And I had — my heart pitter-pattered excitedly against my ribcage, despite promises to my sad-self to be cautious after my last disastrous relationship.

Ingredients, Lisa. I tried to focus my mind where it should be. Good job Adam... *sigh*... had done a round-robin email to the golf club members. At least now I had a rough idea of how many people to cater for. Right, here we go:

Green Soup

Ingredients for 6 portions:

2 cups cucumber

2 green peppers

2 celery stalks

2 cloves garlic

2 avocados

1 large white onion

½ cup fresh, mixed herbs: basil, oregano, chives, parsley, or whatever you have

4 cups vegetable broth

3 tbsp olive oil

3 tbsp Balsamic vinegar

Salt and pepper

1 small chilli pepper

Cooking Instructions:

Divide the vegetables into two piles.

Take the seeds out of the chilli pepper.

Finely cut one pile of vegetables. Throw the other pile, along with the chilli and herbs, into a blender or a big bowl to use a magic wand (immersion blender) on. Slowly add the vegetable broth to the vegetables while finely blending. Also add the vinegar and olive oil. Season with salt and pepper to taste. Divide the soup into soup bowls and decorate with the finely chopped vegetables.

You can eat fresh artisan bread with this, rubbed with garlic, slightly salted and covered in some olive oil. The perfect soup for hot summer days.

52

Duly prompted by the chilli pepper, my mind drifted blissfully off in the direction of Adam again, and the lovely meal he'd so effortlessly prepared at his home, turning down all offers of help, sensibly. So masterful in the bedroom. *Sigh.* Um, kitchen. God, honestly, what *was* the matter with me. A gloopy smile on my face, I reached for the vegetable knife, ticking off each job as I tackled it.

Sigh. "Ahem."

Tum-ti-tum. Sprinkle, sprinkle. "I'm getting good at this, Rambo. What do you reckon?"

"*Squeak, squeak.*"

"Thank you, sweetie."

"I know who I'd like to cover in oil, hey Rambo?" I chatted to my dog in the absence of a certain other available body as I sloshed the soup into Becky's tureen, the bowls not being practical for transportation.

"*Squeak, squeeaak.*"

"Well, he might a bit," I conceded, missing the tureen in favor of the working surface. Whoops. "But I'll try to be gentle with him. Haw, haw."

Ooh, yummy — I had a quick lick of the spoon — tastes yummy. Not as yummy as Adam, of course. *Sigh.* Attempting, yet again, to drag my lewd mind away from my delectable man, I sliced up my artisan bread — previously lovingly hand-crafted... by Becky — and peeled a clove of garlic with which to rub gently all over — the bread, not Adam. *Stoppit.* Then, feeling pleased with myself, I salted the bread lightly, as per instructions, plucked up the olive oil and—

Ding dong went the doorbell. "*Rrroowf, Rrrroowf. Grrrrr. Squeak. Splat!*" went Rambo

—dropped it.

"*Sh... ugar!* Rambo! Come here, sweet... *Eeek!*" Fit Flops, I decided, close to curtailing sexual gymnastics with Adam forever, were not desirable footwear for olive-oil-coated ceramic floors.

"*Hell!*" Reacquainting toes with toebar, I took a tentative step and did a little Buster-Keaton-type soft shoe shuffle. "Just a minute," I trilled as I clutched hold of the working surface and crawled back up the cupboard.

Phew. Well, at least I didn't smack my chin on the way down and part company with my teeth. And at least the bottle wasn't broken, so I didn't have to throw myself bodily at the kitchen door to prevent Rambo coming in and puncturing his little paws. So now what?

Righting myself on my feet, I contemplated my next step.

Drrriiing went the doorbell.

"Coming!" I yelled as Rambo went into muffled, "*Squeak, grrrooowwwf,*" overdrive, zoomed around in a circle and then skidded toward me.

"No! Rambo, stay!" Drat, too late. Rambo ice-skated clackily across the kitchen floor, did a perfect figure-eight, then landed like Bambi, legs splayed and Piggy still feverishly gripped in his mouth.

"Baby! Oooh, shit. Stay! Don't move, sweetie. Mommy's coming." Kicking off Fit Flops, I squelched carefully toward him for fear of slipping again and flattening him. "Are you all right, sweetie, hmmm?"

"*Rrrowf?*"

"Aw, babe." Careless of greasy knees, I dropped down beside him and plucked my puzzled JR up. "Has Rambo got an oily tum, then? Poor baby. Naughty floor." Hands under armpits, I held him high and peered under his piggy to survey damage to belly, and...

Rat-a-tat-tat came a tapping at the kitchen window. Honestly, some people. I mean, is there no privac... Oh... *miGod!* "Um, hi. Little accident," I mouthed.

"Major frickin' catastrophe," I mumbled, tucking a wriggly Rambo under my arm and knee-walking across the floor.

Cupboards for support, I levered myself up the sink-unit and peered over the taps to see Adam's snooty mom peering back.

"He-*lloo,*" I trilled and beamed her a bright, if slightly imbecilic, smile.

Her Maj blinked at me bemusedly.

"Yes?" I asked, and waited. I wasn't entirely sure what else *to* say. I mean, what had she come for apart from to measure me up to Adam's perfect, but sadly deceased, wife, Melissa, and find me lacking, no doubt.

Her Maj gestured to the door. "Can... I... come... in," she mouthed, sloooowly.

Haw, haw. You must be joking, missus. I really must look mentally challenged if she thought I was fool enough to let her in here to inspect my kitchen. The state it was in at the moment, I might as well send Adam a goodbye text and drown myself in the soup.

I gestured to Rambo. "Sorry." I shrugged, bobbing him plus Piggy up and down. "I've just oiled my dog."

Hah, that's foiled her I thought, satisfied, as Her Maj opened her mouth and closed it, clearly lost for words.

Or not. "Lucy," she said, obviously realizing a pane of glass did not make a sound barrier. Also obviously not realizing Lucy was *not* my *name*, "I do worry about you, you know?"

Rambo, who up until now was either unaware of or too stunned by the apparition at the window to react, stiffened and peered startled at her over his pig. "*Grrrrrr...*"

"That's so sweet of you, Isabelle." I smiled uber-sweetly. "But really, there's no need. You obviously already worry *far* too much about Adam." That last bit was just too hard to resist.

Isabelle pursed her lips, apparently unimpressed.

"Did you want something? It's just that I have loads to do. You know, for *your* golf club do?"

Reminded of her priorities, Isabelle composed her mouth into a semi-sweet smile. "Ah, oui," she said. "I just wondered..."

"Sorry?" I knitted my brow, following her progress as Her Maj teetered curiously to one side. Oops, I think her stick just sank in my carefully cultivated mud-bed.

Isabelle straightened herself huffily back up. "I said," she shouted, "I was just wondering how your valiant attempts in the kitchen were going?"

"Ah, magnifique... ily," I assured her French... ily, and gave her a thumbs up.

"...*Rrrrowf, grrrowf.*" Clearly perturbed by the accent, Rambo wriggled — and... *Uh, oh...* piddled.

And his aim was spot on. I froze as Isabelle's mortified eyes followed a trickle of pee down the window.

Oops. "Sorry." Attempting to whip the embarrassing origins of the accident out of sight, I twizzled on the spot, Rambo and Piggy in arms. "He gets a bit excite..." I started to explain, but the words got wedged in my windpipe.

There floating atop my *Green Soup* was an un-vegetable like, white, sphere-shaped object that definitely didn't belong there. Oh, no... my eyeballs nearly plopped in after it.

Rambo's Piggy, I had a sinking feeling, was one squeak short of three.

And Her Maj was definitely not amused.

"Unbelievable," she muttered. "I really do wonder about Adam's judgment sometimes." So saying, cuttingly, she turned to huff haughtily off, her progress hampered a bit by her stuck-in walking stick.

"Cow." I felt my cheeks flush with humiliation. I was quite tempted to skate to the door and invite the old trout in after all.

So, do I just fish the squeak out, start again, or tell Isabelle to go to hell?

Start again, I decided, after a shuddery few breaths. She-witch mother or not, I was not going to give Adam up without a fight.

Mom, it had to be. I ignored my cell phone, and my nuisance parrot's impression of it. I'd have to ring her back, but right now I needed to concentrate on the food.

The *Chilli Peppers* I'd prepared without major disaster — and only one threat to remove the middle from Flint's bell. Those were in the fridge and good to go. All Lisa had to do was lob them in the oven for fifteen minutes, then sprinkle with the shallot and cheese.

Right, next... I ran a forearm over my brow ...*Olivia's Pride*. Let's hope Lisa still had some pride left when it was served.

Olivia's Pride

Ingredients for 4 portions:

12 lasagna sheets

1 cup chopped tomatoes (fresh or canned)

2 cups leaf spinach (fresh)

1 cup Greek yogurt

½ cup cream

½ cup parmesan

2 tsp butter

Salt, pepper, nutmeg

Cooking instructions:

Mix the Greek yogurt with cream and shredded parmesan.

Grease an oven dish and turn your oven to 200°C. Wash the spinach and let it drain well. Cut off the hard ends and discard these (or feed them to your bunny).

Mix the spinach with tomatoes and season with salt, pepper and nutmeg.

Layer lasagna sheets, spinach mix and yogurt sauce into the oven dish — make sure you end with yogurt sauce.

Bake this for 40 minutes in the oven and serve with a tomato salad.

Cripes. So what was so complicated? Didn't need a genius, did it, *a la moi?*

Feeling pretty pleased with myself, I whistled over to the oven with the dishes (I had doubled up on the ingredients to make two lasagnas. A pretty neat achievement, considering two boiled eggs were normally beyond me) — and discovered a small hitch in *The Plan*.

"Crap." I fiddled with the oven knob. Then fiddled with the timer. Then noticed a hand sign, which looked basically like a stop sign, and fiddled some more, and swore, "Frickin' hell! Frickin' thing! Why *now?*"

"*Frickin' hell. Frickin', caw, caw.*"

Ignoring Flint, I headed for the miscellaneous drawer to find — no oven instructions. "*Grreat!* Frickin' marvelous!" Frustrated, I slammed the drawer closed, dragged my hand over my neck, trying to figure out what to do next, then groaned as there was a knock at the door. "Guess who?"

"*Grreat, Frickin'... Squaawk.*"

Despairing, I walked into the hall to see a familiar silhouette through the glass in the door. "*Frickin'* Mother." Who else? "Interfering old..." I stopped and counted to three, before I muttered something I might regret.

As much as I wanted to tell myself this was all Mom's fault, in honesty I couldn't. If anyone was to blame, it was me. I should have held off introducing Mom to Lisa, preferably until after the honeymoon. I should never have gone along with this golf club thing. I *knew* deep down Lisa had only said yes because she'd felt obliged to; to please me. I should have told Mom to get professional caterers in. Told her to butt out of my life, and done with.

Sighing, I pulled open the door and turned to walk back up the hall.

"Adam," Mom limped on in, "about Lucy. I..."

"Lisa," I grated.

"Yes, Lisa." Mom followed me into the kitchen. "Darling, are you sure she's not a little bit... How does one put this delicately? Retard..."

I don't frickin' believe this. Temper dangerously close to the surface now, I retrieved my dishes from the oven and clanged it shut. "A little bit what, Mom?" Banging the dishes down on the table, I faced her full on.

Obviously looking as furious as I felt judging by the surprised expression on Mom's face. "Adam, I know you like her," she said after a second of composing herself, "but she really is rather peculiar."

Counseling myself to stay calm, I folded my arms — and waited.

"She talks to her dog."

"Right." I nodded. "And I talk to Flint."

"*Squawk. Zip it. Zip it. Caw, caw.*"

Take heed, Mom, I thought angrily.

"Yes, but..." Mom fiddled with her beads. "There's really no way to tell it other than it was, Adam, so I will." She notched up her chin, bracing herself to tell whatever terrible thing she had to. "She oils it."

"Oils what?" I was not getting the drift, I have to admit.

"The dog, Adam, obviously. She oils..." Mom stopped, her eyes darting worriedly this way and that "...its willy."

What!? I laughed, utterly bamboozled.

"And before you accuse me of looking for faults, not only did I see the evidence with my own eyes, but Lucy told me, quite blatantly. 'I've just oiled my dog,' she said, and then the horrible little gremlin peed all over the kitchen window."

"*Rr*right." I shook my head, bemused. "Well, that was some achievement for a mouse-sized dog. Mind you," I paused to ponder, "I think I might pee a fair distance if someone oiled..."

"Adam! This is no joking..."

I cut her short. "And you were?"

"Sorry?"

"Where were you, Mom, that you were able to see the evidence with your own eyes?"

Mom looked a touch uncomfortable. "Looking through the window," she admitted, sheepishly. "I had knocked on the door, of course...."

"Ahh." I turned away to look for my car keys.

"...but Lucy didn't answer."

"I'm not surprised."

"I'd only stopped by to check..."

"Exactly!" I turned despairingly back to her. "Lisa might not have wanted to be 'checked' on, Mom. Did this occur to you? Her telling you she'd just oiled her dog was probably her way of (telling you to eff off, I didn't say) saying she was busy." Mind you, I actually wouldn't be that surprised if Lisa had smothered Rambo in baby oil, I have to admit.

"I, er..." Mom's attention seemed to have drifted off somewhere. "Adam," she glanced around, taking in the various ingredients and general pandemonium, "what on earth?"

"I'm helping *Lisa* out." I enunciated the name, located my car keys and a handful of shopping bags in which to scoop scattered ingredients, then went back for my lasagnas. "She has rather a lot of work on her hands, you *might* recall."

"But..." Mom glanced worriedly around again "... Adam, you can't cook. Melissa always did all the cooking. "

"*Caw, caw.*"

Jesus. "I know!"

Mom looked shocked now.

"I know, Mom," I said, more quietly. "But I'm trying, because I care about Lisa. And I know you're trying, too, to look out for me, but I need you to..."

I trailed off as Mom paled, visibly. Live your own life, and leave me to live mine, I wanted to say, but couldn't.

"Look, Mom, do you think you could please... you know, just go? We'll talk... later."

"Well..." Mom puffed up her chest feathers indignantly. "If I'd known Lucy wasn't up to the job, I would never have asked her." She turned, muttering toward the door. "Melissa would have had it all cooked and catered for by now. And she certainly wouldn't be oiling a dog in the kitchen."

God give me strength! That was it. I'd had it. Trying hard to stay calm, I opened my mouth to tell her politely where to go, and...

"*Frickin' Mother. Squaawk. Interfering old... Caw, caw.*"

Chapter 6 Guaranteed To Make You Drool

"Becky, this is Luke," my neighbor, Madge, introduced her nephew proudly.

And proud she might well be. Oh, *yum-my*. Be still my fluttering eyelashes.

Down, girl. I tried not to drool on his shoes, while taking in the all-over suntan and pecs that would make rugby players too embarrassed to come out of the showers.

"Pleased to meet you," Luke said, an Aussie twang to his accent, and beamed me an ultra-white smile. Ah, so he was weather-tanned, rather than salon-tanned, then? Ooh, sexilicious. He could drag me off to Bondi Beach anytime.

"I'll leave you to show Becky your zoom lens, Luke," Madge said coyly, and all but pushed the photographer through the door. "Don't get carried away and coat him in chocolate, Becky. Her *Cassatta Seduction* is to die for." She waggled her eyebrows suggestively, then tottered off, leaving Luke standing uncertain in my hall.

"Ahem. So," he flashed me another bone-melting smile, "where do you want me?"

Now there was a leading question. "The kitchen, I think, don't you? As it's food we're photographing." I gave him a knowing smile back and led the way.

"Pity," he said, hitching his bag up on his shoulder and following me through.

My eyes pinged wide with surprise. Well, he was a bit full of himself, wasn't he? *Humph.* How utterly crass, Neanderthal and... totally ego-boosting. Chat away, I say.

"Oh, incidentally, did you know there was some guy hanging about downstairs?" Luke said, behind me. "Asked me to let him in when Aunt Madge buzzed me up, but I wasn't sure he was very desirable."

Ryan, again, I supposed. 'That'll be my ex, and he's not," I assured

Luke, leading him over to the table, where my *Cassatta Seduction* and *Avocado Fudge* stood. "He's trying to win me back."

"Oh?" Luke peered through his viewfinder. "And is he likely to succeed?" he asked, fiddling with his camera, i.e. not looking at me, which probably meant he was making conversation, rather than being interested in me. Not that a man who probably had to step over the entire female race falling at his feet would be.

"Not unless he has a personality transplant, no."

"Ah, right, so..." Luke idly snapped off a few shots "... does this mean I *might* be in with a chance, then?"

'Scuse me? My mouth clanged unbecomingly open.

"Sorry. I, er..." He glanced at me — nervously? "It's just Aunt Madge said you'd split with your boyfriend and... well, I've seen you around a few times, and I, er..." He trailed off as I stared at him, stunned.

"Sorry," he said again, with an awkward little shrug. "You're probably not interested. Forget I said anything."

Oh my God. I closed my flabbergasted mouth. He was for real. "Well, I might be," I said, composing myself and opting for demure, rather than sweeping the desserts from the table and forcing his body down on it. "Depends."

"On?" he asked hopefully.

I wiped my finger nonchalantly around the aluminum foil. "How well you use your equipment, obviously." Ugh, I cringed inside. I could not believe I'd just said that.

Luke laughed. "Er, now, what would be the right answer, I wonder?" He pondered, a mischievous twinkle in his dreamy blue eyes. "I've had no complaints yet?"

"Pleased to hear it," I said, feeling myself go weak at the knees.

"Pleased to please you." He smiled his easy smile again and stepped toward me. "So do you want to..."

Ooh, yeah. My tummy flipped excitedly over.

"...tell me about the food?" With which he reached for my hand — and sucked so sensually on my chocolate-coated finger, my knees almost buckled and gave way.

"*Cassata Seduction,*" I croaked.

"It's doing it for me," he said softly, his lips now a mere whisper from mine.

I closed my eyes, puckered up wantonly, wanting him, held my breath, and... "It's very cold out here." ... almost fell face first into the cake as a voice drifted up the hall.

Ooh, God! "Ryan! Go *a-way*."

"I forgot my coat," Ryan said petulantly through the mailbox.

Luke raised an enquiring eyebrow. "The undesirable ex?"

"Very," I growled, stomping toward the front door.

"So what's this called?" Luke asked after the second dessert, clicking away with his camera as I came back into the kitchen.

"*Impress the In-Laws,*" I said glumly.

Luke smiled. "Not his parents, I take it?" He gestured toward the living room, where Ryan was busy dismantling the sound system, having decided to reclaim his DVD player as well as his coat.

I rolled my eyes. "Most definitely not. I think Ryan's parents stopped being impressed the day he was born."

"Ouch!" Luke laughed. "I take it your splitting wasn't amicable, then?"

"We weren't on the best of terms when Ryan left, no." *Wearing my Red Soup starter,* I fancied it prudent not to disclose.

"Come on, forget about him." Luke nodded me over. "Tell me about this fabulous food. More importantly, what goes into making it."

"Why?" I asked, surprised. "I thought we were just going to take photos of the finished dishes, not what goes into them."

"Ah, but what goes into them is important. A few artistically arranged ingredients next to the dish creates an interesting, artsy composition; draws the eye in, if you like."

"Oh, right." Yes, I could see that. He obviously knew his stuff, being the 'artsy' sort with faded jeans that flattered in all the right places... very nice, ahem, biceps. Hair, truffle-colored, sun-kissed and sexily curly. The sort of hair you just itch to run your fingers through and...

"A beautiful cook doing her thing on the website would most definitely draw the eye in." Luke gave me a slow wink and clicked in my direction.

...canoodle him senseless.

"What thing?" Ryan asked suspiciously, standing at the kitchen door, arms full of Blu-rays, DVDs, and trailing wires. "What website?"

"Avocados," I addressed Luke.

Luke looked puzzled. "Avocados? Supposed to be an aphrodisiac, aren't they?"

"Correct," I informed him knowledgeably. "The Aztecs first ate them to enhance sexual performance, apparently."

"Intelligent as well as beautiful and a fantastic cook. Wow!" Luke whistled appreciatively. "So when do you fancy getting married?"

"I'll check my diary." I giggled, over a clang as one of Ryan's DVDs hit the floor.

"They have some kind of potent property, then?" Luke asked, setting up his tripod as he talked.

"They're supposed to have loads of nutrients essential to sexual health," I went on, reveling in Luke's unashamed flattery and attention, especially in front of Ryan, who'd practically hyperventilated at mention of the M word, "including beta carotene, magnesium, vitamin E — sometimes called the sex-vitamin. Some people call it the chocolate of the fruits, and see it as a remedy for sexual... you know... problems."

"I can see why mom-in-law would be impressed." Luke smirked.

I blushed.

Ryan flushed, furious. "Becky, could I have a word please? *If* you can spare a moment, of course."

"Certainly. Goodbye," I obliged.

"So what other magic ingredients go into producing this gastronomic delight?" Luke asked.

Ignoring Ryan, I turned to fetch my ingredients list from the working surface. "It's actually a remarkably simple recipe," I said, liking this new 'sharing' experience with a man. "Here you go."

Impress the In-Laws (Avocado Fudge)

Ingredients for just enough fudge for your in-laws and maybe one piece for you:

3 avocados

½ cup butter

4 cups unsweetened cocoa powder

4 cups confectioners' sugar

1 cup white chocolate chips

optional: pistachios for decoration

Preparation:

Line a 9 x 11-inch pan with greased wax paper.

Cut the avocados in half and remove the pits. You can use a spoon if the pit is too slippery to grab. With a spoon, scrape out the flesh. Melt the butter in a large saucepan over low heat. Place the avocado flesh and melted butter in a high mixing bowl. Blend with a magic wand (immersion blender) until the mixture is smooth. Scrape the mixture back into the saucepan and stir over low heat.

Add the cocoa powder and stir until you have completely worked it in.

Stir in the sugar a little at a time. Make sure that the sugar has completely dissolved into the mixture before adding more.

Pour the chocolate chips into the mixture and quickly mix them in.

Remove from the heat.

Pour the fudge mixture into the prepared pan.

Chill in the refrigerator for at least 1 hour and then cut into squares.

Lightly press a pistachio onto each fudge piece for decoration.

"Three avocados?" Luke commented, reading over my shoulder, his cheek close to mine, his citrusy, oaky aftershave playing havoc with my will to resist biting him. "I think I'll have me a slice of that."

"Do you need it?" My eyes slid interestedly sideways. *A little nibble on his earlobe possibly?*

"Not sure." His mesmerizing eyes met mine. "Do I?"

"Ahem!" Attention-seeking, again, Ryan coughed from the doorway. We read on.

"Cripes," Luke blew out a breath, sending goose bumps down the length of my spine, "that is really simple. Reckon even I might be able to tackle that. So what about the preparation?"

"Easy as pie," I told him confidently and showed him the preparation instructions.

"...and make sure you leave some for others," I finished.

"Or make two?" Luke suggested, now dangerously close to slurping distance.

"I already did," I assured him headily.

Luke smiled his sex-loaded smile, sending a prickle of pleasure from my nose to my toes. "Clever girl."

Yes, and flattery will get you absolutely everywhere. *Mmm, but he was gorgeous, like profiteroles drenched in fresh cream, and mine for the eating. Slurrrp.* I tried to stop my tongue hanging out.

"Becky," Ryan snapped, rudely interrupting my fantasy. "A quiet word, if I..."

"You've had one, mate." Luke cut him short. "The lady said goodbye. Now, would you like me to give you some assistance finding the door?"

Ryan drooped out for the absolute last time, his plug trailing sadly behind him, as I was going into the preparation of my *Poseidon Serves Up* and *Cheese Cream Ahoi*. The latter — main ingredients being Camembert, very ripe, and cream cheese — Luke confided, was seriously whetting his appetite.

"Mine too," I confessed, extremely close to licking his lips, when — as Murphy's law would have it — my cell phone rang.

"One sec," I promised Luke, noting Lisa's number and picking up. "Hi, Lis... sweetie, where are you?" I cocked an ear, as Lisa's voice reached me over running taps and flushing water.

"Oh, right. She's in the bathroom, washing her dog," I whispered to Luke aside, who was looking a bit curious. "He's got oil on his little winky."

"Just wiggle it about a bit," I went back to Lisa. "You'll soon get the hang of it."

Luke's eyes shot wide.

"Hands-free," I explained.

Luke nodded — and furrowed his brow.

"She's having trouble with her *Drunken Chicken*," I filled him in, as Lisa's frantic tones crackled in my ear. "Run out of oil, apparently."

"Ah, right." Luke now looked utterly confounded.

"Oh, hon, sorry... I would drop you some over, you know I would, but I'm busy arranging my bits and pieces for the photographer."

"Pardon?" I blinked at Rambo, who blinked back, shocked — though more at having his bits dunked in lukewarm water than at what bits Becky might be arranging for the photographer, I suspected.

Well, well, she'd obviously got shot of layabout, freeloader, Ryan then? At least I assumed she had, since I heard her ask huskily, *'so how do you want me, posed or au natural?'* as she'd hung up. *Haw, haw.*

"Come on, sweetie." I reached to pluck my bedraggled baby out of the bath before he got doggy pneumonia. "Let Mommy give you a quick rub down with your lovely, fluffy towel, hmm?"

Rambo, obviously not fancying being rubbed down with anything, turned into a miniature Houdini, wriggled out of my arms in one second flat, then bolted along the landing to hide under the bed.

Aw, cute. He looked like a little drowned rat. I peered in after him, attempting to coax him out, before dashing off in search of olive oil.

"Come on, sweetie. Look, chewie!" I waggled a treat and made a smacky-lip face.

Rambo made a *'do I look stupid'* face, and stayed firmly put.

"Squeakie, hon! Come on!" I squeezed Piggy excitedly.

Rambo, rather less excitedly, plopped his damp snout on his paws and ignored me.

Ah well, at least it was cozy under there. Sighing, I was shuffling back out, when my new hands-free cell phone — unobtrusive to wear, but still got tangled in my hair — beeped in my ear. "Adam!" I said delightedly, followed by, "Ouch," not so-delightedly, as my head made contact with the mattress supports above me.

"Where are you?" Adam asked. "You sound a bit muffled."

"Under the bed," I muffled, spitting dust balls.

"Rrright," Adam replied, after a pause. "That bad, hey?"

"That bad," I assured him.

"Look, I'm on my way over. How about I help you on top of the bed and kiss it all better?" he asked, his tone sexy and sultry and so uber-suggestive I'd probably end up molesting him before he got through the door, if I had time of course, which — I glanced at the bedside clock… eeek! …I most definitely hadn't.

"Lovely," I said distractedly — and a bit frantically. "Do you think you could do me a huge favor and bring some olive oil?"

"Erm…?"

"For the *Drunken Chicken*," I clarified, skidding to the bathroom to make myself halfway presentable, then doubling back downstairs to leave the door on the latch. "I was going to do it there, but now I'm going to do it here," I explained, panting a bit as I went. "But it'll be stone-cold-sober at this rate."

"Got you." Adam laughed. "Not. Lisa, you're special, did anyone ever tell you that?"

"Sorry?" I would have given my cell phone an odd glance, but it was fetchingly wedged in my ear.

"In the best possible way," Adam went on kindly, thank God, "and utterly adorable, and I love… talking to you."

Wow. I paused on the landing, feeling as if my heart had grown little butterfly wings. That was quite the nicest thing any man had ever said to me.

"Ditto," I sighed, doe-eyed, then skidded on. "The front door's on the latch. Watch Rambo doesn't slip between your legs, won't you? Oh, and watch the floor. I'm upstairs cleaning the oil out of the bath."

Taking shopping bags first, I tentatively nudged open the front door, watching out for Rambo slipping between my legs — I shook my head. Lisa might be peculiar, but that's exactly what I loved about her. I made my way to the kitchen shouting "Hi, just me, Adam," as I went, lest I give Lisa apoplexy.

Not entirely sure why I had to watch the floor, I studied the carpet underfoot in the hall, which looked pretty immaculate, and the kitchen floor looked so shiny you could... *ShooOOT!* "Ouch!!" ... scrape your dinner off it.

Crap! Stunned for a second, I groped a hand around hoping I hadn't squashed anything essential, like the Oreo cookies, then snatched my head from the tiles as Rambo attempted the kiss of life.

"Hey, small-fry." Easing myself to a sitting position, I plucked him up. Rambo was still determined to stuff his tongue in my mouth and wriggled, and, "*Grrrowf,*" yep, piddled. He then slithered like a well-oiled eel out of my grasp and shot back to the hall.

And another pair of jeans bites the dust. I sighed and got to my feet, or tried to. *Damn,* that hurt. I grimaced, a hot pain slicing through my ankle, as Lisa flew through the door.

"OhmiGod! Adam! What happened?!" Planting her hands firmly under my armpits, Lisa tried to bear my weight. Given she was about five-four to my five-eleven, it was no mean feat, but she managed it, somehow.

"Couldn't work out what I was meant to be watching on the floor." I winced, as she helped me to the safety of the working surface. "So I thought I'd take a closer look."

"Oh, God.... Olive oil. I dropped it when Her Maj... your mom rang the doorbell and..." Lisa trailed off, chewing worriedly on her lower lip.

That would explain Rambo's oily willy predicament — I hid a smile.

"Ooh, *stupid* me. I'm so sorry, Adam. Does it hurt very much? Let me see." Lisa dropped promptly to her knees and tugged at my sneaker.

Arrgh, yes! "No." I gulped. "No, it doesn't. It's fine. Honestly."

I'd sustained a fair few injuries intervening in late night brawls while on duty. It was sprained, not broken, I guessed. Lisa didn't need to feel anymore guilty about it than she obviously already did.

"Are you sure?" she blinked nervously up at me, tears brimming in her huge green eyes. And I knew then, without doubt, that I loved every one of her gorgeous peculiarities. I... loved her, unquestionably.

"I'm fine," I assured her, my throat tight and my heart playing a steady drumbeat in my chest. "More than."

"Now," I coughed, and tried to concentrate on what I should be doing here, rather than what I'd like to be, "much as I like women throwing themselves at my feet, we have cooking to do. Come on. You can throw *me* on top of the bed and kiss it all better later, yes?"

"Promise?" She smiled as I helped her to her feet.

"*Oh*, yes," I promised, most heartily. "Where's Rambo?" it occurred to me to ask as we limped toward the hall.

"Upstairs. He hid under the bed after I..." Lisa glanced at me and stopped.

I glanced from her to the open front door — and my heart stopped dead. "*Jesus...* Rambo?!!"

Adrenalin numbs the pain and stimulates blood flow to the muscles and the brain, according to the duty-doctor at the station. Whatever, I didn't feel a thing as the adrenalin kicked in, launching me across the road.

I didn't think, other than one thought, as Lisa screamed, "Stay, Rambo!!" behind me; that thought being: I had to move a hell of a lot faster than the JR - and the oncoming car.

It was definitely a case of love me, love my piddly JR I realized as I pulled Lisa hard toward me.

"He might have been... hiccup... squished," she said, bravely trying to hold back her tears.

"Ahem." I glanced down to where Rambo was sandwiched between us, his rapid heartbeat so close to mine I could feel it.

Lisa laughed, thank God. "Thank you." She sniffled, and ran a hand under her nose.

"No problem." I wiped a tear from her cheek.

"I should have thought to..." we both said together.

"...drop the latch," I finished.

Lisa nodded. "Sorry." We did it again.

"Adam, there's something I need to... tell you." Lisa glanced down, then hesitantly back to me — and from the look of trepidation I caught in her eye it had to be something serious.

Crap! My own heart skipped a beat. I eased her chin up, my emotions skidding off kilter. "What, Lisa? What is it?"

"I can't do it, Adam!" she blurted.

"Do... what, exactly?" I asked warily.

She fixed me with her huge eyes. "This," she said nervously.

"Right. I see." I sucked in a breath and nodded. My turn to be brave now I supposed, even though I felt a part of me had just died. Almost murdering her dog aside, I'd messed up monumentally by introducing my mother and my ghosts into a relationship that had barely got started. "I, erm... Okay." I swallowed, hard. "Well, I can't say I blame you. I..."

"I want to, but I'm just no good at it."

I shook my head. *Christ*, Becky had warned me, but... was Lisa's self-esteem really that low? "Lisa, that's bollocks," I said bluntly. "You're a fantastic..."

...beautiful woman I was about to say, when Lisa went on, "You're a much better cook than I am. I'm just totally crap at it."

"Sorry?" *Cooking?* She was talking about cooking? *Jesus.*

"I mean, I can cook... a bit," she added quickly, "but..."

I stared at her. She looked at me, blushing furiously. "I'm not very good at the, um, catering bit. I should have said. I know I should have, but with Her Maj... your mom having her operation and everything... And now I'm in an awful mess, and I'll end up letting her down, and I'll never be able to hold my head up again, and..."

I laughed, hugely relieved. "You have to be joking?"

Lisa knitted her pretty brow. "I'm not, Adam," she said quietly. "I've committed myself to this, and now I can't do it, and I'm just going to feel awful."

And her self-esteem would sink even lower. Uh-huh. Sure. Now was my opportunity to come clean about my non-existent culinary skills. But for Lisa's sake, maybe it would be better to get through this and then start over, honestly.

"Erm, just a suggestion, but how about we pool our resources and be totally crap together? The plus side has to be *Her Maj* won't ask again."

Lisa blinked at me, then stood up on tiptoe and leaned in to kiss me.

"*Rrrrowf. Pant, pant.*"

I got a mouthful of Rambo's tongue.

Adam's *Olivia's Pride* was in the oven. The timer was set. We had forty minutes and counting to prepare the *White Soup*, before tackling the *Drunken Chicken*, by the end of which Adam will have either limped out the door with vague promises to ring, sometime, or have been consumed, whole. *Sigh.*

"Right," he studied the ingredients list.

I studied him.

White Soup

Ingredients for 4 portions:
1 pound white asparagus
Salt, pepper
4 tbsp butter
2 cups milk
3 tbsp crème fraîche
1 slice of smoked salmon

Peel the asparagus and cut it in slices about 1 inch long (or 3 cm, essentially bite-sized).
Melt the butter and add the asparagus, frying it for a few minutes.
Add the milk and cook on low heat for about 20 minutes.
Season with salt and pepper.
Serve in deep plates and garnish with a dollop of crème fraîche and some diced salmon.
Serve with fresh bread.

"A breeze," he said, holding out his hand surgeon-like. "Asparagus."

"So masterful," I sighed, again, passing him the asparagus and not minding fetching and carrying for this man one little bit.

He smiled, embarrassed.

And obviously modest. *Sigh.* Dreamy-eyed, I passed him the other ingredients.

"Okay, so we..."

Sigh. "You'd make someone a happy wife, you know?"

"Yeah." Adam smiled and gave the soup a final stir. "Do you think Rambo would want to marry me though, that's the question?"

"Ooh, definitely. He's selecting his wedding dress as we spea... um?"

Chapter 7 Mixed Messages

He hadn't meant anything by it. I tried to concentrate on finding my missing *Drunken Chicken* recipe. It was a knee-jerk reaction to my saying he'd make someone a lovely wife. Panicked at where the conversation might lead, Adam had scrambled for something to say and ended up proposing to my midget Jack Russell. It was no big deal. Except it was, because now we were avoiding eye contact.

God, what had I been thinking? The first months of a relationship should be easy and fun, carefree and light-hearted. Men are attracted to women who are sassy, independent and confident, according to Becky. Not clingy, needy, and looking for commitment from a man to fix things. So far he'd witnessed me having a nil-confidence, near-nervous breakdown, an attention-seeking asthma attack, and then I'd topped it off by bringing up the heavy M-subject before he'd had chance to draw breath after the first kiss. The man was probably ready to run a mile. But he couldn't, of course, hobbling around my kitchen as he had with a bag of frozen peas stuffed down his sock.

"Cute," he'd said, hurriedly dropping his gaze after my conversation-stopping comment about Rambo selecting his bridal attire, "but I see him as more a top hat and tails sort of man myself, hey, Rambo? So, little guy," he'd petted Rambo then, desperate to look anywhere but at me, "who's the lucky girl then?"

In answer to which Rambo had "*Rrrowffed*," delighted, then — stump wagging manically — galloped into the living room in search of his current crush, squeaky Piggy; leaving Adam and me with an unusual silence hanging between us. Adam clearly felt awkward — and I couldn't blame him. It was ridiculous to think that now the subject had come up he might pursue it, but... I had a sneaking suspicion that if things didn't work out between us, this time the man wouldn't leave with a little bit of my heart. He'd take all of it. Break it. Because this man so easily could.

We'd barely spoken since, though we were both otherwise occupied searching for the chicken recipe, which mess-of-a-life-me had managed to misplace.

"Have you tried the trash?" Adam asked, dragging his hand over his neck as he limped over there.

Poor thing, he looked so tired. He was obviously in pain and probably totally fed up. I wouldn't be surprised if he did dump me once the dreaded golf club do was over; by email, probably, or text. Or Twitter, so he could keep it short: @LisahrtsRambo Sorry, babe. Nice knowing U but not that nice.

"Yes." I sighed. "And the trash can, and the compost can. I've checked the living room, the bedrooms, Rambo's bed, bathroom, handbag, coat pockets, washing machine... I'd better ring Becky, I suppose."

Marshaling my sassiness, I selected Becky's number and stuffed my hands-free in. Better to have Becky sighing despairingly in my ear than Adam's mom looking grimly down her nose, I supposed. Adam was still looking everywhere and anywhere but at me.

"Honestly, Lisa..." Becky sighed despairingly when I explained my dilemma. "You really do need to get organized, you know, sweetie."

"I am organized," I countered defensively, padding across the newspaper adorning the floor, which was still soaking up spilled olive oil, and — *squeak* — inadvertently stepping on Piggy. At which Rambo emitted an excited "*Rrrowf, rrrowf*," and plucked Piggy up to give it a jugular-ripping good shake, unfortunately at about frozen pea bag level.

"*Arrgh! Shhhi...*" Adam paled and scrunched his eyes shut.

"Adam!" I flew after him as he did a sort of hoppity-hobble across the floor.

"*....ooOOT!*" He blew out a breath as he clutched the back of one of my shabby-chic chairs for support, his forehead beaded with little droplets of sweat.

"Oh, God! Are you all right?" I asked, flapping uselessly around him. Stupid question.

He rolled his eyes. "Yeah, bruised but not beaten." He mustered up the tiniest of smiles.

"Are you sure?" I chewed worriedly on my lip, almost expecting him to hop right around and straight out the door.

"Fine. Nothing a triple brandy and a shed-load of pain killers wouldn't fix. Joking, Lisa." He shook his head, as I blinked, alarmed. "It's not so bad to make me suicidal, promise."

Yet I thought, noting the look of exasperation in his eyes.

"Go on," he said, gesturing me back to my call. "Becks will be wondering what's happening."

"Unsurprisingly, knowing you, Becky's not," my absolute best friend, shortly to be demoted to ex, commented wittily in my ear. "Adam still in once piece, is he?" The last was said with loaded insinuation, I noted.

"Meaning?" I asked, feeling a bit miffed. It wasn't as if I'd grabbed him on purpose, was it, with a view to chaining him to my bed... cooker.

"Nothing," Becky said, all innocence. "I just couldn't help wondering whether you might have *accidentally* slicked him in oil, too, and..."

"Dropped him?"

"I was going to say, *dragged* hi..."

"Well, I haven't." I cut her short, feeling quite incompetent enough. "I take it you've dropped Ryan?" I asked, alluding to the photographer Becky had been arranging her bits and pieces for — no doubt, uber-efficiently — and steering the subject away from Adam... and oil.

I glanced wistfully over to where he was sitting at my ancient Ikea table, looking down and dishevelled; dark shadows under his sultry brown eyes, indicating he was definitely tired. I so wished I could drag him — ever so carefully — upstairs, wrap him up in the blanket and kiss him all better.

Later, I busied myself trying to find the working surface. I'd make him lie back, relax, and I would slick him all over — with massage oil, rather than olive. That's if he wanted to, of course. Did he? I snuck another glance, to see Adam raking his hand through his hair. In despair?

He caught me looking, smiled uncertainly, then dropped his gaze.

And my heart dribbled miserably into my tummy. I'd finally met the most caring, sensitive man I was ever likely to meet, and I'd scared him off. Overwhelmed him with my all too obvious insecurities and unintentional hints at commitment, and now he was contemplating how he could extract himself from the nightmare of all new relationships, I just knew it.

"Well, wouldn't you?" Becky reminded me she was still there. Talk about self-centered. I mean, there's just no future with a man who's more excited by South Park than sex, is there? Not that there was going to be a future with someone who paled at the mere mention of marriage, in any...

"Yes, I've got a pen," I trilled over her, hoping she'd get the hint and get off the subject. "Somewhere."

Question was, where? I fumbled in drawers and around working surfaces, finding everything from green beans to leftover asparagus, which didn't write very well, but no pen.

"Got one," Adam said, limping across to me, painfully, I noticed. I so wished he would stay sitting down, if he wouldn't lie down.

Becky obviously got the message. "Oh, right, hold on a sec. I'll just get my copy of the recipe."

Relieved, I waited, smiling gratefully at Adam who'd managed to find some paper amongst the mayhem.

"Coffee?" He made cup gestures, flicked the switch on the kettle when I nodded, and offered me a smile back. The look in his eyes wasn't the smiley one I was used to, though. It was one of disillusionment. Oh, God. I closed my eyes, wondering if I shouldn't just make it easier for him and suggest he should go.

"So..." Becky came back on line "... do you think you and Adam might... you know... do the deed?"

"Ahem!" I threw Adam another smile, trying to look light-hearted and carefree, and coughed again, but a tad more daintily. "Bit of a cough," I croaked, as he looked at me perplexed, and missed the mug with the water.

"*Crap,*" he muttered moodily, and not at all Adam-like, shook the dribbles from his good foot, and reached around me for the dishcloth.

"I didn't mean imminently, obviously," Becky went on blithely in my ear, "but you have to admit, Adam is excellent baby-making material. You'd be mad not to jump at the chance of marriage if he..."

"Ahem, ahem, *ah-hemmm!*"

Adam looked at me, alarmed now, and patted my back — and did that lovely toe-tingly massage thing with his hand. "Okay?" he asked with concern in his delicious, chocolaty brown eyes, more the man I was familiar with, felt comfortable with.

"Course," Becky trundled on, "I'd have to be chief bridesmaid."

Arrrgh! "*Shhh...* ugar!" Where was her off button, for God's sake?! Adam was practically nose-to-face with my thingy. He'd bolt for the door, feet or no feet, in a minute.

"Sugar?" he said, with an askance glance, and reached for the pen and paper.

"No, no. Um, not sugar, but thanks for offering to write the ingredients down, Adam," I grated through gritted teeth, "since you're so CLOSE to hand."

Becky was quiet for a nanosecond, then, "Ahh," she said, "got you. Right, well, you have all the ingredients, obviously, as you've shopped for them, but I'll just run through them again. Here we go."

Becky reeled them off. I repeated them, and Adam, clearing a less soggy place on the working surface, dutifully wrote them down.

"He is a bit yummy though, isn't he?"

"Yes, he's standing right next to me, writing them down verbatim." I slid my eyes toward Adam, and smiled again, inanely.

"Oops."

"Thanks, Becky. You're an absolute star. I owe you." I sighed, relieved, despite the still impossible task ahead of putting the ingredients together.

"Chief bridesmaid," Becky hissed. "But no puffball dresses. And definitely not lemon, makes me look sallow. Oyster blue's good. I'll do the cater..."

She stopped, mercifully, a male voice interrupting her flow before I was forced to fall in a dead faint or throw myself out of the window.

"This cobbler dish sounds interesting. Is it made up yet?" the man asked, cobbler pronounced 'cobbla'. Definitely not Ryan. Definitely sexy.

"Oops, gotta go," said Becky gaily, no prizes for guessing why. "Services required elsewhere."

"So, I gather." I smirked. "Photographer still in one piece, is he?"

"Not when I've finished with him," Becky growled. "Byeee."

Honestly, the girl was incorrigible. She'd have him dribbled in chocolate and devoured before his shutter clicked.

"All good?" Adam asked still smirking as I turned.

"Absolutely, as far as Becky's concerned," I assured him. "She's got herself a new yummy boyfriend, it seems."

"Only as far as Becky's concerned?" Adam eyed me quizzically.

"Well, obviously not as far as Ryan's concerned," I answered, though a bit puzzled at the question. "But, let's face it, he was about as exciting as tapioca, and moody. I think Becky regretted allowing things to get so serious, but wasn't sure how to tell..."

Drunken Chicken

Ingredients for 4 portions:

2½ pounds chicken (your favorite parts)

4 tbsp tomato paste

2 tbsp Dijon mustard

4 cloves garlic, chopped

1 cup chopped tomatoes (fresh or canned)

1 tbsp paprika powder

2 branches each thyme and rosemary

2 tbsp olive oil

1 tbsp flour

2 cups wine, dark red (Shiraz or Merlot, whatever you intend to serve with dinner)

4 shallots, halved

2½ cups mushrooms

1 French baguette

2½ cups green beans

Cayenne pepper to taste

Cooking Instructions:

Rub the chicken parts in salt, pepper and flour. Fry them on high heat in olive oil in a very big pot. Add tomato paste, mustard, garlic, tomatoes and paprika powder as well as herbs. Cover the chicken in wine — if you need more than 2 cups, that's fine too, it will make a great sauce for mopping up with bread. Leave covered on medium heat for about an hour. Make sure you regularly come back and check on it.

In the meantime, you can cut the ends off the beans and fry them. They taste much better fried than cooked, so fry them on low heat in a little olive oil and add some cayenne pepper. They will need about 10 minutes.

Cut the mushrooms in half and add to the chicken about 10 minutes before serving. Serve with French baguette and the fried beans.

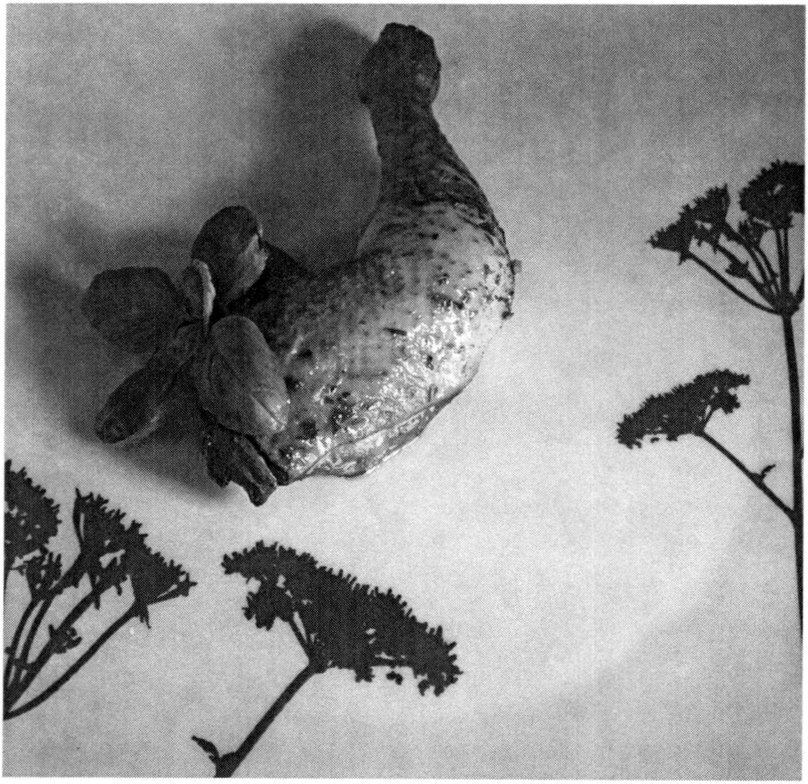

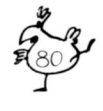

OhmiGosh. I blinked from the menu to Adam as he handed it to me. He'd doodled a little smiley face on it. That had to be a sign. It must be... but... it was a sad little smiley face.

"So, erm..." Adam took a huge breath and ran a hand through his hair "... you're okay, then?"

"Me?" I blinked at him. "Yes, of course." Uh, oh, was he looking for a lead in? About to smile, relieved, then say *good* followed swiftly with *bye*? I gulped, and blundered airily on. "Apart from being a complete pain in the butt, of course, but..."

"No, I didn't mean..." Adam cut in, now looking definitely exasperated. "I meant you and..." He stopped and glanced at the ceiling, then back at me. No trace of a smile in his eyes now. No tummy-melting, smoldery sexual innuendo. He was deadly serious. "Lisa, do you want me to go?"

Oh, no. My heart twisted inside me. My inclination was to blurt *no!*, but I couldn't get the word past the lump in my throat. Hesitantly, I asked, "Do you want to?" quietly instead.

Adam didn't speak. Just looked at me.

Don't you dare. Don't you dare. I braced myself and willed my traitorous eyes not to cry. "I mean, I do think you should, because of your foot. You shouldn't be hobbling around on it. You should be tucked up in bed."

"Now, there's a thought." Adam's mouth curved into a small smile.

"But I don't want you to go, no. Not unless you want to."

"Right." He paused while I studied the oily newspaper underfoot. "Well, I don't."

I started breathing again.

"So, shall we cook? And then maybe talk, yes?"

"Yes." I nodded, and swallowed.

"We make a great team." I glanced sideways at Lisa, as she passed me the Shiraz.

"Do we?" She looked alarmed. Not quite the reaction I'd hoped for.

"I... thought so, yes." Glumly, I chucked the wine over the chicken, though I quite fancied chucking it down my throat. What the hell happened? One minute we're doing okay, or at least I thought so, and the next... well, judging by the body language and the conversation on the phone, Lisa apparently didn't feel the same way. "Don't you?" I plopped the lid on the pot, reached for the pan — and fished like mad in the absence of a clue what else to do.

Lisa passed the olive oil, carefully, then reached for a knife, looking anywhere but frickin' at me. Why wouldn't she look at me?

Great. I heaved out a sigh and passed Lisa the green beans, which were my side of the working surface. "I take it that's a no."

"No!"

"Shoot! Lisa!" I caught hold of her hand, as she took a swipe at the beans with the knife and almost shaved off her nails. "Careful," I warned her, trying a smile, which she missed, so fast did her eyes flick to mine and then away.

Lisa continued swiping at the beans, making me seriously nervous. "I do!" she said. "I mean…"

And there it was. The great, big, crappy elephant in the room. Words around a subject Lisa had inadvertently brought up, and then looked as if she'd quite like for the ground to open up.

I had tried to make light of it, noting her panicked expression. Okay, I'd been fishing a bit then, too, when I'd glibly wondered whether Rambo wanted to marry me. Backfired a bit, I thought ruefully. Lisa had stared at me as if I'd just announced I wore women's clothing.

She'd been acutely embarrassed.

No wonder, judging from the coded conversation on the phone, she'd already discussed where our relationship was headed with Becky. Women did, I supposed, do the girl talk thing. I had no problem with that. I just wished she'd talked to me, would talk to me.

So what now? Ask her outright? Play for time? Or walk… limp away. My ankle was killing me, but losing Lisa… that was going to hurt a hell of a lot more.

What I couldn't fathom was why she was putting herself through this catering for the golf club do charade if she *was* considering dropping me. Pride, possibly? It just didn't add up.

"Lisa…" I relieved her of her precisely-trimmed green beans, tossed those into the pan to fry, and decided to take the bull by the horns.

"… do you, erm…?"

Yep, well done, Adam, very decisive. Do you *what*, ferchrissakes? Want to see me anymore? Like me? Love me, a little? Could you learn to, maybe, hopefully? *Jesus.*

"Could you, erm…" I amended awkwardly "… pass me the cayenne pepper?"

"Oh." Lisa's huge eyes clouded with uncertainty. Well, at least she *was* looking at me I supposed. I wish she didn't look so temptingly kissable every time she did though. "Yes, right," she said, reaching for the pepper.

"Mushrooms?" she asked.

"Better added about ten minutes before serving," I informed her knowledgeably, having written down, ergo read, the instructions.

Lisa sighed. "I am *so* glad you're competent in the kitchen," she said, and started to clear away her cut-ends of beans, no cut-ends of fingers in there with them, thankfully. "I'd have been lost without you."

That got to me a bit, I have to admit, given I was about to get 'dropped'. I sprinkled the pepper over the beans and banged the pot down. "Lisa," I started, determined now to get cards on tables, and then leave, I guessed, hopefully with my dignity intact, "I think we need to…"

"Ooh, clever boy!" Lisa cried delightedly over me. "He's found his big prickly!"

"Scuse me?" I swung around to see Rambo trying to nudge through the cat flap, a huge rubber appendage gripped horizontally across his mouth, unfortunately hampering his progress.

"His prickly bone," Lisa enlightened me. "He lost it in the grass, didn't you, hon, hmm?"

Figured. Rambo was so short he could lose himself in the grass. I smiled as Lisa put down her tools and scooted over to the door to allow dog plus appendage entrance.

"There you go, baby. Come on, let's show Uncle Adam, shall we?" She scooped the dog up, nuzzling his ear as she did, which was about the only bit of his face visible.

I couldn't help but laugh as Lisa carried him over nestled in her arms. "Cool… erm, prickly, Rambo," I said, giving it a playful tug.

"*Grrrrrrr.*" Rambo clearly wasn't sharing.

I stroked his spotty chest, careful of a certain other appendage, which I reckoned was aimed at about eye level.

"*Grrrrrrr.*" Spit. "*Grrrowff.*"

"Oooh, naughty Rambo," Lisa said, kissing his snout as the prickly plopped out of his mouth, and clearly striking fear into the JR's heart. "Uncle Adam only wants to play."

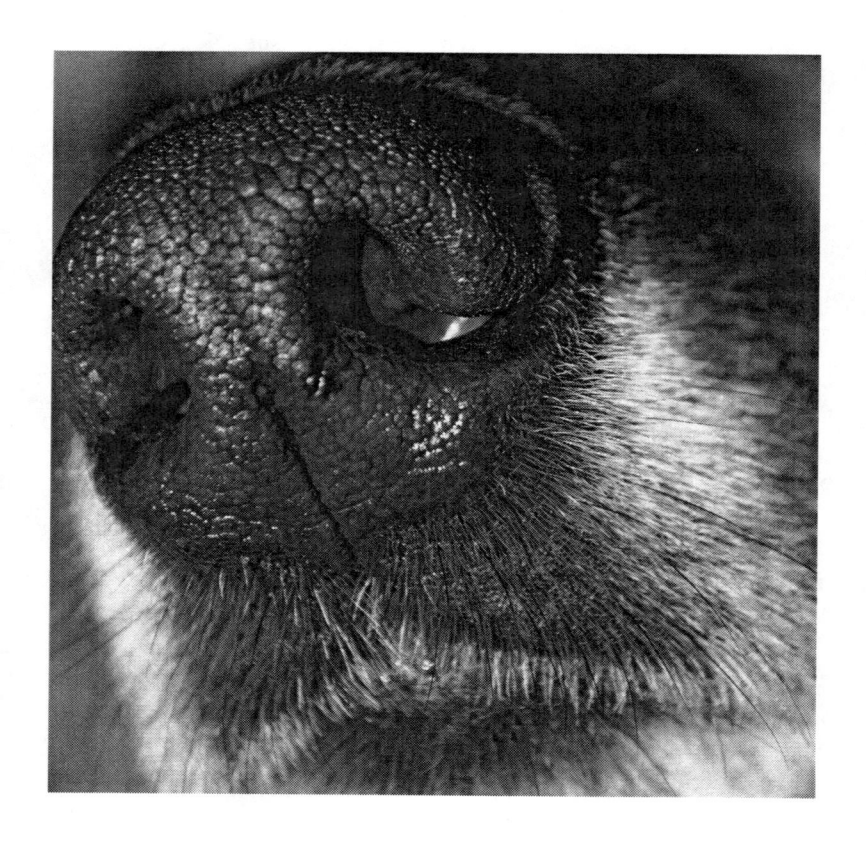

"It's okay," I assured her, retrieving the rubber toy from the floor and handing it back to its wriggly owner a bit quick-ish. "We'll play fetch later when he's less excited."

"You're lovely." Lisa gave me one of her sparkling smiles, and I so wanted to cup her face in my hands and tell her she too was lovely and lovable. Probably not a good idea with Rambo's prickly between us.

"But not as lovely as Rambo," I suggested, as she gave him another cuddle. Jealous? Of a dog? Me? Yeah, I was a bit then, actually. "He really is your baby, isn't he?" I risked another stroke of his tiny chest.

"Absolutely." Lisa blinked at Rambo adoringly, whose *Grrrrrrr* sounded a bit gurgled, he having cottoned on that if he opened his mouth the toy came out.

"Cute," I said, then took a breath, and another risk, a huge one. Well, if I had something to lose — a lot to lose — I figured, better now than later when the hurt might cut deeper. "You, erm, don't want children then?"

"Oh, yes," Lisa said, still gazing down at her cross-eyed JR, "of course I do, when..." She stopped, and looked at me with something akin to bewilderment in her eyes.

Meet the right man. I filled in the gaps, then counted silently to five — in tandem with my heart, which was hammering so loud in my chest, I swear to God I could hear it.

"Um..." Lisa ran her tongue over her lips.

Don't do that. Please don't do that. I tried to swallow but my throat was too dry.

Lisa glanced away, then back. "I mean..."

"I think I need to go," I said quickly. "The, erm, *Zebra*, chocolate pudding... thing. I forgot the, erm, yogurt. I..."

"I have yogurt," Lisa said staring at me, stunned now. "Loads. A whole fridge full. You don't have to go all the way..."

"And the Oreos. I forgot the Oreos," I lied. I could have cried. I could feel my heart cracking, actually feel it, as I watched Lisa's eyes filling up. Because she'd hurt me? Oh, Christ, was I hurting.

I looked away. "I'm on duty," I said, "later. I'll be there though, at the golf club. We need to find time to talk, Lisa, when this... idiotic do... is over. That's if you want to?"

I didn't wait for Lisa to answer. I really needed to go.

Chapter 8 Bitter Sweet Love

"No, Mom, I won't be seeing Lisa again before the do." *Or ever again, once the darn do was over.* That thought weighing heavy in my chest, I wedged my cell phone moodily on my shoulder while I pulled fresh ingredients for the *Zebra* from the shopping bag.

"Well, you can ring her, can't you?" Mom wouldn't let up on whether or not Lisa would be serving decaf at coffee time, apparently crucial to the golf club do being a success. Crucial what with Mom being Lady Chairman, ergo determined to impress.

"Look, Mom, I'm busy right now," I said, by way of avoiding further inquisition. "I have to go to work later, and I..."

"Running around for Lucy, I suppose."

I eyed the ceiling, exasperated. *No, scraping my bloody heart from the floor,* I didn't say. The last thing I needed was Mom clucking sympathetically while wearing her *I told you so* face, then rambling on about my wife being a hard act to follow.

"Her name is *Lisa*, Mom," I told her for the billionth time, not that it mattered anymore. "And I'm not running around for her." I didn't lie. I was more limping, thanks to the oil slick on Lisa's kitchen floor. "I offered to help out, so..."

"Melissa would have had the whole thing organized like a military operation," Mom went on, tutting and clucking disapprovingly. "She certainly wouldn't have roped you in and had you rushing around and then going on duty half-exhausted."

Yep, there she went. No disrespect to Mel — God rest her — but I really had had it with this. First off, if I'd volunteered to do a bit of the 'rushing around' back then Mel might *not* have been rushing around, therefore might *just* have been driving more carefully. Secondly, *if* Mom hadn't made it so glaringly obvious she had Melissa way up there on a pedestal, Lisa would never have tried to measure up, offering to cater for a do she hadn't got a snowball in Hell's chance of pulling off single-handedly — and then maybe Lisa and I would have stood a chance. Yeah, and maybe the cow flew over the moon. Things were what they were. Obviously I just didn't do it for her.

Still didn't need this though, not now. I just wanted to get on, get the golf club do over with — and then move on... without Lisa. I swallowed back a tight lump in my throat. "If you wanted the thing run like a military operation, you should have got professional caterers in, Mom, don't you think?"

"Well, yes..." Mom sounded a bit sheepish. "But Lisa did offer."

"Because you were about to have your knee operation," I reminded her. "She's doing this out of the kindness of her heart, Mom." I defended Lisa, because despite her 'dropping' me, and obviously having discussed my merits — or lack of — over curry with her friends, she did have a kind heart, I was sure of that. "Now, did you want something else? I really have to..."

"Be a darling and text her then, Adam. It's just that I have so much to do, organizing taxis, and then I have to get myself ready, which is a task in itself when one's still relying on a crutch for..."

"Look, Mom, it's *your* do. If you need to discuss anything with Lisa, just ring her." I reeled off Lisa's number, then stopped. Yes, Lisa had hurt me, more than she would ever know, but did I really want to inflict my mother on her again? Uh, uh. As much as I would prefer to right now, I could never hate Lisa that much. "I'll do it. I'll text her."

"Thank you, darling. I knew I could count on you, at least." Mom huffed, demonstratively, no doubt itching to start on about Lisa being odd, or peculiar, i.e. not frickin' perfect again.

"Is there anything else?" I asked, dumping the last of the ingredients on the working surface and sneaking an Oreo cookie. Despite having cooked enough food to feed an army — well, it felt like it to someone who'd previously needed a compass to find the kitchen — my stomach was beginning to think my throat had been cut.

"Well..." Mom pondered. "I did wonder, while you were there earlier, at Lisa's, whether you might have noticed anything... strange, at all."

Christ, she didn't give up easily, did she? She'd already got Lisa down as a psychopath who hid decapitated bits of fish in strange places and sexually abused her dog. What was she going to dream up now? "Strange how?" I shook my head, despairing.

"In the soup," Mom went on, not very enlighteningly.

Nothing to do with olive-oiled willies, then? I smirked as I took a bite on my Oreo, recalling Mom's face as she'd recounted how she'd supposedly witnessed Lisa oiling her Jack Russell's bits, mouthing the word willy as if one might leap out of the shadows and bite her. "Such as?"

"Eyeballs," Mom imparted.

Jesus... What!? "Eyeballs?!" I choked, utterly incredulous.

"Floating in the soup," Mom elucidated, mind-bogglingly.

"Oh, come on, Mom..." I laughed, then, *"Ouch!"* bit my tongue. "You hath to be joking, right?"

There followed a pause, one loaded with indignation if ever I heard one. "Do I sound like I'm joking, Adam?"

"Erm, no." I tried to straighten my face, which was almost impossible with Flint parroting hilariously from the living room, *"Eyeballs, eyeballs. Squaaawk. Caw, caw."*

"No, you don't. So..." I pulled in a breath "... eyeballs..."

"In the soup."

"*Rrright.* So, was it fish-eye soup?" I enquired, the deep pass way too hard to resist.

More silence, then, "Adam! You really can be heartless sometimes, you know?"

Yeah, that'd be because someone broke it, I thought wryly.

"Peering into one's handbag to find a decapitated fish head peering back is *not* amusing."

"Ahem. No, sorry."

"It was *very* traumatizing. An extremely peculiar thing for Lucy to do, and not something one wishes to be reminded about."

"*Squaaaaawk. Eyeballs! Caw, caw.*"

Hell! I pressed the phone to my chest. "Flint! Zip it! Her Maj is not amused."

Silence ensued, thank God, as I went back to the phone, face straight, voice in serious mode. "Sorry, Flint's a bit hyper. You were saying?"

Stony silence this time. Obviously I couldn't see her, but I could feel the vibes, even over the phone. "Mom?" I wondered if she was still there.

"Nothing important, darling." Mom continued, sniffing stoically, which spelled trouble. "Don't you trouble yourself worrying about me."

I rolled my eyes. *After I've given birth to you, given up my life for you, etc, etc.*

"I'm sure you have more important things to do than trouble yourself with my trifling concerns."

Now I felt guilty. How did she *do* that? This do was all about *her* for Christ's sake. "Mom, I don't have... well, yes, I do have things to do, but... look, I know this is important to you, Mom, but..."

"I have to get on now and get myself organized anyway," she went on over me, "if only I could just... reach... my... crut..."

Crap. I tensed as I heard a thud, followed by a metallic clatter in the background. "Mom? Are you all right?"

Silence.

"Mom?!"

"Yes, I'm... *pant, pant, wheeze...* fine, darling," she came back on the phone. "My crutch fell, that's all, but I managed to *struggle* down and *crawl* across the floor to reach it. Go on, you get off."

"Right." I heaved out a weary sigh. "If you're sure you're okay?"

"Perfectly sure," she replied chirpily. "I'll just go and try and make myself presentable. It might take a while, of course, what with my hair to wash and my *tiara* to polish!"

With which Mom plopped the phone down, leaving me suspecting I must just have put my foot in it.

"*Chrrrist*, frickin' women!" Frustrated, I reached for yet another recipe. I tried, I really did, but even with the benefit of telepathy I don't think I'd ever understand what women really wanted.

"*Caw, caw. Chrrrist, friggin', caw, caw.*"

"Flint, one more, just one more word and you're trussed and stuffed, end of."

"*SquawwwK!*" Flint nutted his bell.

"Eyeballs in the soup, ferchrissakes," I mumbled mystified. "What next? Piranhas in the frickin' decaf?" Pity it hadn't been a piranha Lisa's piddly JR had dropped in her handbag, I thought agitatedly. Then felt guilty again. Mom was lonely, I knew, but she really was enough to try the patience of a saint. Little wonder Lisa had opted to bail out before things got too serious, which they apparently hadn't for her, despite the amazing connection between us. At least, I'd thought there was. The mind-blowing sex, which it obviously wasn't for Lisa.

Dammit. Trying to keep the emotions in check, I flapped open the recipe, determined to get on with the job at hand and get this thing over with, probably severing the only real connection between us, Her Maj's flipping golf club do.

Zebra... I read... (chocolate pudding with yogurt served in a cocktail glass, layered to look like a zebra, with a cookie).

Right, so... I helped myself to another Oreo... here we go, again.

Zebra

Ingredients for 4 portions:

½ cup starch (potato or corn)

4 tbsp sugar

4 cups milk

½ cup chocolate (to taste, dark is visually more effective for this dessert)

1 cup yogurt

4 Oreo cookies

Mix starch with the sugar.
Take 10 tablespoons of the milk and mix this with the starch and sugar to get a thick paste.
Cook the rest of the milk with the chocolate so that the chocolate melts.
Once it has boiled boiling, take it off the heat and stir in the starch mixture.
Bring to a boil once more and take off the heat. Let cool for about 10 minutes, stirring occasionally to avoid the building of skin. If skin does build, eat it or discard it, but do not stir it into the pudding.
Fill into glasses, layering it with the yogurt to achieve the zebra look. Let cool completely and decorate with an Oreo cookie right before serving.

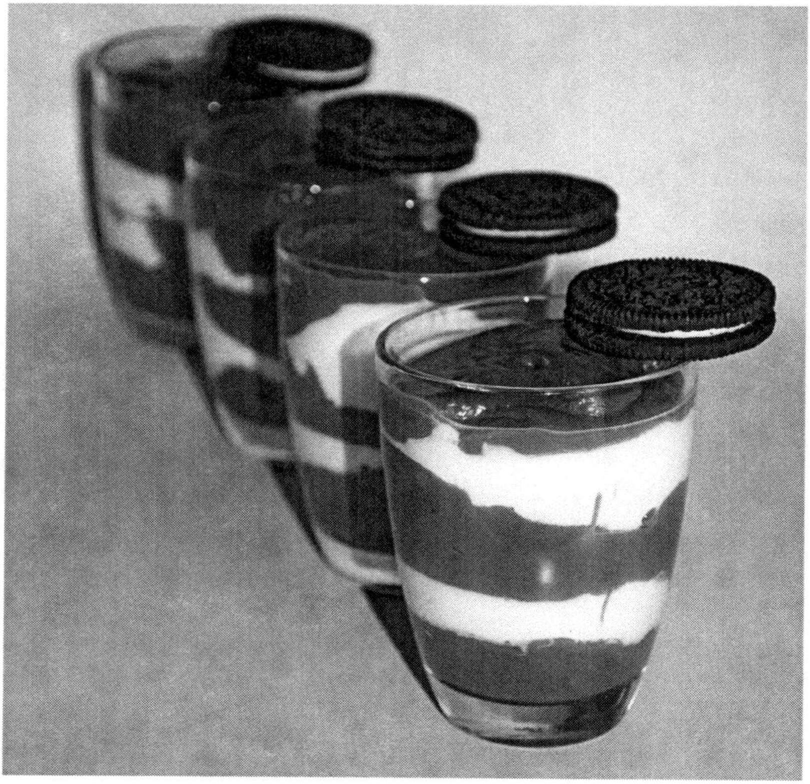

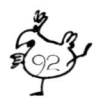

"Check."

"*Check, caw...*"

"Flint, I really do *not* need an echo. Okay!"

"*...Caw.*"

Well, that was reasonably idiot-proof, apart from some idiot eating the Oreos, meaning I'd have to pick up more on the way to the golf club to deliver the *Zebra*, which I'd have to do in uniform, I supposed. At least it would be a good excuse to get the hell out of there again though, before I was tempted to confront Lisa and demand explanations, which would look pretty pathetic.

But then, maybe I should. Debating, I ran a hand over my neck, then reached for my cell phone and selected her number. We could end on reasonable terms, couldn't we? I could wish her well and ask if we could still be friends, maybe. Yeah, right. Pathetic.

Having a reasonable excuse, I opted to text instead. If Lisa wanted to text me back, she would. If she didn't she wouldn't, but at least this way I wouldn't have to suffer the added humiliation of her noting my number and not picking up.

Okay, so, thumbs shaking a bit, I started:

Hey Lisa. Sorry 4...

Sorry for what? Leaving so suddenly? Feeling as if I'd just had the crap kicked out of my heart? Falling in love with you? I backspaced.

Hey Lisa. How R U?

Ecstatic, obviously. I backspaced.

Hey Lisa. Mom wants to kno...

Idiot.

R U Serving decaf 2nite?

Not a lot of point adding Xs, I left it at that and hit send.

"It's all right, Rambo. It's not you, sweetie." Dragging my hand under my snotty nose, I tried to reassure my crestfallen midget JR.

Oh, God, he did look like a mouse now. A sad little mouse, his pointy ears had flopped, his stumpy tail had flopped, his piggy had plopped from his mouth to lie in an abandoned heap on the floor. "Don't be sad, babe. It's not you. It's Mom... m... m... me! *Wah!*" I dashed over to pluck poor Rambo up and gather him to me.

Rambo's ears boinged worriedly up. He blinked at me, startled, then stoically set about trying to fix my leaky face with his tongue.

I'd done it again! I couldn't believe it. Tried too hard and fallen in love too soon, too hard. Offered myself to the man of my dreams, body and soul — and he didn't want it.

Pulling in a shuddery breath, I looked around at the chaos where once was my kitchen. So what did I do know? Throw the dishtowel in? Or carry on catering for his she-witch mother's golf club do, suspecting, as I did, it was a test she'd set me knowing *I* would fail miserably.

I cradled Rambo tightly to me, not caring that Adam thought he was my baby. He was. Granted, Rambo might not be tall, dark and handsome with a sex-loaded smile, a lovely toned chest and taut stomach with hair in all the right places that disappeared tantalizingly below belt level... *sigh*... and sultry, liquid chocolate-brown eyes that just oozed... scratch that. Rambo's eyes were much sultrier and what's more: Rambo's eyes didn't lie.

Rambo was loyal and faithful, and loved me — Goddess-gene deficiency and all. What's more: he was always there when I needed him. Not running... limping like greased lightning for the door at the mention of the dreaded M word.

Adam had already been married, I was well aware of that. He wasn't likely to want to plight his troth again to the first person he'd properly gone out with, I supposed. Particularly when he'd been plighted to perfection personified, which his mom had been at great pains to point out. That's probably what enlisting my help with the golf club fiasco was all about: to show me up. Prove I couldn't measure up. Obviously I didn't measure up for Adam either, in bed or out.

Sniffing sadly, I kissed the top of Rambo's soft, furry head, who — being attuned to my mood — indulged me and didn't wriggle or piddle at all. Bless.

Well, forget it. I might not be perfect, but I would *not* give up; to do that would be to fail. I'd be lying if I told myself I didn't care whether I lived up to anyone else's expectations, to Adam's. If I was to salvage anything from this disaster though, namely my self-esteem, I didn't want to fail me.

Okay, so sassy, independent and confident didn't come naturally, but clingy and needy wasn't me either. Screwing up I was good at, particularly when it came to choosing men; screwing them I might have been good at, but cooking I was totally not good at. But I could do this — I had to — I would not give Her Maj the satisfaction!

Chin high and shoulders back, I stood tall, then, "Oops, sorry babe," apologized to Rambo, who, with his snout nuzzled in my cleavage, was looking a bit squished.

As for Adam — I plopped Rambo gently down on the oil-sodden newspaper still adorning the floor — I would never speak to him again, ever. I wouldn't ring him, wouldn't text...

Bleep, bleep went my cell phone.

Unless he texted first, of course.

Nonchalantly, I dove across the kitchen to grab my phone. It was him. My eyes seized on Adam's name, glowing like a beacon of hope in the incoming text box. Was he sorry? Did he want to see me? Declare undying love for me? Eagerly I read the text, my battered heart bouncing buoyantly from the depths of despair.

"Oh." I read it again, disbelieving, but it still said, *R U serving decaf 2nite?* No love, no Xs, no smiley. Nothing. My heart deflated like a pricked balloon.

"Right. *Sniffle.* Fine. *Ahem. Sniffle.* We don't care, do we, baby?" Blinking hard so as not to plop more fat tears on Rambo's head, I plucked up Piggy, gave its two remaining squeaks a sharp squeeze, then hurled it across the room for him.

"*Rrrowf, rrrowf. Thanks, Mom,*" went Rambo, then, little legs scrambling frantically, dashed off to hunt it down and kill it.

Well, whatever, the show would go on. *Sniffle.* I reached for a yard of kitchen roll, had a hearty blow, and then steeled myself to delve in Adam's shopping bags, forgotten in his rush to leave. No menus, I noticed, but the ingredients were there, including the yogurt and the Oreos for the *Zebra* he'd said he'd left at home.

"Bastard," Becky pronounced without ceremony when I recounted my further missing menu dilemma and the reasons why ever so calmly.

"Who is?" I heard her hot food photographer in the background.

"Hold on, hon. I just have to quickly liaise with Luke," Becky said. "Won't be a sec."

There followed a muffle, then, "Adam," Becky answered Luke, her hand obviously over the mouthpiece, but not very well. "Spineless little... but he's so nice. I really don't get it."

"What, the guy who's already been hitched?" Luke asked.

Well, they'd obviously been having a good old confab while Becky arranged her bits and pieces for him. I had a little nibble on an Oreo while I waited.

"Probably wants to play the field a bit," Luke suggested, presumably knowledgeable on the subject. "Can't blame the guy."

Then silence, apart from crunching and gnashing my end as I stuffed another Oreo in my mouth. I was waiting for Becky to give her hot photographer one of her killer looks, which no doubt she would be from under her luscious lash extensions.

"Now me, I'm a one woman kind of guy," he went on in a dead sexy Australian twang, "as long as that woman is you."

Gulp. My Oreo slid chunkily down my esophagus. Sighing wistfully I reached for another, the munching on which might at least drown out kissy lip sounds.

"Sorry, Lisa." Becky came back on, breathlessly. "Luke wanted to discuss the positioning for the *Jammed in There*."

"Pardon?"

"My marmalade," Becky expounded, while I licked miserably at a middle bit. "So," she said with a sigh, which at least wasn't despairing this time, "you're determined the show will go on then, regardless?"

"Yes." I nodded determinedly. "It's a self-esteem thing, you know?"

"Good for you, hon. Don't let the bastards grind you down," Becky said sounding pleased, until Luke photographed my culinary catastrophes, I suspected. "Okay, if Adam makes a *Chockfull of Zucchinis* too, that's tough. Yours is bound to be better anyway... possibly."

Thank you. My bolstered self-esteem drooped a bit.

"Right, got a pen?"

"Yes," I assured her, eye liner pencil confidently poised in place of the pen Adam had obviously pocketed. Me, need a man? Never.

Chockfull of Zucchinis

Ingredients for one cake (8-10 slices):

½ cup olive oil

½ cup butter

1¾ cup sugar

2 eggs

2½ cups self-rising flour (OR 2½ cups of regular flour with 1 tsp baking soda)

½ tsp salt

¼ cup cocoa

½ tsp cinnamon

½ tsp vanilla bean marrow (stick the scraped bean into your sugar or ground coffee container for flavoring)

2 cups zucchini (peeled and grated)

Baking Instructions:

Preheat oven to 200°C.

Grease a 9x13 inch baking dish or a bread loaf pan big enough for a 750g bread. Swirl one teaspoon of flour around the dish so that it is entirely covered in grease and flour. This will help you get the cake out of the pan later.

Combine oil, butter, sugar, vanilla and eggs in a big mixing bowl.

When smoothly mixed, add the flour, salt, cocoa and cinnamon (and baking soda, if necessary) a bit at a time, until all is mixed evenly together.

Add the zucchini and combine to make an even dough.

Pour into the pan and bake for 35 minutes.

You can make a similar cake with carrots instead of zucchini, with or without the cocoa, depending on your preference, and with some lemon zest. You can also leave out the cinnamon and use more Christmassy spice mixes when baking this later in the year.

Use the recipe as an inspiration and see what you can come up with!

Sniffle. Sniffle.
"Easy as pie," I repeated Becky's stock phrase. "Definitely." *Sniffle.*
"Lisa," Becky said softly, "are you crying, sweetie?"
"Uh, uh." *Sniffle.* "Absolutely not."

Lisa hadn't texted me back. No surprise there; I didn't really expect her... "*Shoot!*"
I fumbled for my ringing cell phone as I was halfway out the door on my way to work; prison duty probably, with my damaged ankle, being serenaded by some sad, inebriated dimwit who fancied himself as Elvis. Better than staying home alone though, dwelling on what might have been.
It wasn't Lisa. Noting Becky's number, I tried to hide my disappointment and answered the call, "Hi Becky. What's up?"
"What's up? What's up?!" Becky said, sounding remarkably Flint-like. "Bastard!"
"Erm, right. Nice to hear from you too, Becks. Would you like to enlighten me as to why you're giving me ear cancer? Or am I supposed to guess?"
"Don't give me that clueless man crap, Adam," Becky growled. "Like you don't know very well what you've done."
"To?" I asked warily.
"Lisa!" Becky barked. "You remember? The woman you slept with and then dumped before the sheets cooled down?!"
"Whoa, hold on a minute." That was completely backwards. "Becky, what the...? *I* didn't do any dump..."
"Oh, no, of course you didn't. I forgot, you didn't have the balls to do that, did you? You just walked out the door without even so much as an explanation!"
"I... what?" Now I was getting totally confused. "Becky, I... look, it's complicated. I didn't... It's not the way it seems."
"No," Becky scoffed. "It never is, is..."
"Becky, if you just give me..."
"You men, you're all the same."
"Becky, please can I get a word..."
"Predictable, that's what. I don't know why I thought *you'd* be any diff..."

"Becky, shut up!"

"Charming."

"Thank you," I said as Becky finally, mercifully went quiet. "Is she all right? Lisa, is she…?"

"No, she is *not* all right! She's not crying!"

Not… erm…? Nope. I scratched my head, definitely clueless now.

"So, what *did* you say to her?"

"Nothing." I scrambled through my brain for exactly what *had* been said, and by whom. "I mean… she… Lisa made some jokey comment about wedding dresses. Then she was embarrassed, thinking she was giving out wrong messages, I supposed. I could see she was, so I… well, to be honest, I didn't know what to say. Then she talked to you on the phone and I…"

"God, Adam! Idiot. Go and talk to her." Becky plunked the phone down.

… heard her saying she hadn't dropped me *yet…* didn't I?

"*Squawk. Frickin' women. Caw, caw.*"

Chapter 9 Romance on the Rocks?

My dodgy ankle being a bit of a hindrance should a hot pursuit be called for while I was out on patrol, I guessed I'd end up pulling prison duty. And my scintillating company for the next few hours? Freddie Mercury, no less.

Great. I sighed, as the suicidal football fan, obviously having drowned his post-match blues in booze, rhapsodized me with another few bars of Queen's mammoth hit.

"*I see a little shilhouetto of a man,*" he slurred, one eye closed and reeling where he sat. "*Scaramouch, Scaramouch, will you do the Fandang...* going to shleep." He trailed off, his other eye giving into gravity and his upper torso keeling dangerously toward me.

"Uh, uh, not that way, sunshine." I straightened him up, and leaned him in the direction of the cot. "Don't want you cracking your head and bleeding all over the cell floor, do we?"

"*I shometimes wish I'd never been born at all,*" the guy picked up with heartfelt gusto.

"I know how you feel, buddy." I tried to unhook his arm from my neck, before I ended up locking lips with the guy. "Not worth crying over though, hey?"

"He mished the goddam'd goal!" The guy caught hold of my collar. We were now eyeball-to-eyeball, and his were well-bloodshot and tellingly red-rimmed, I noticed. "A whole goalmouth he'sh got to go out and he hitsh the frackin' bar!"

"Tragic, dude. Truly tragic," I sympathized. "You win some, you lose some, tho..." Uh, oh. Alcohol consumption dictating, the guy finally flopped drunkenly backwards with yours truly sprawling embarrassingly on top of him. *Christ.* I'd end up sleeping with the bastard in a minute.

"Nice and cozy in there, I see, Adam," my sergeant called wittily from the desk, as I tried to extract myself from my predicament. "Want me to close the door and give you some privacy? Haw, haw."

"Fun-ny. Not." Not overly amused, I managed to disentangle myself, unfortunately not before the guy burped out a lager breath that could strip the paint from the walls. It was definitely going to be one of those shifts, I decided, trying hard to hold on to my patience.

"Thanks," I muttered, curling a lip as I straightened up and wondering what the frickin' hell I was doing here. It was Lisa I wanted to get up close and personal with, not some inebriated old fart. Why hadn't I taken a sick day, got my backside back over to hers and tried to talk to her, rather than skirting around the issue?

We'd had a misunderstanding that was all, not even an argument, ferchrissakes. I'm not sure Lisa was capable of arguing her corner. She should have done. Should have belted me over the head with the frickin' *Drunken Chicken* and topped it off with the Shiraz. What was I thinking skulking off like a sulky six-year-old because I'd thought I might not be the one she wanted to share her future with?

I didn't deserve to be the figure in her future if I wasn't prepared to fight for her.

Dammit, I needed to ring her. I glanced at our cell guest who was snoring steadily now, sleeping it off, thank God.

"Go on, Adam, go grab a coffee," my sergeant said, mercifully, behind me. "I'll keep an eye on Freddie here."

"Thanks, Chris. I owe you." I ran my hand through my hair, relieved. "I'll just check his airway. Don't want the guy choking if he puke... oh, for fu..." Patience now not overly abundant, I eyed the ceiling as the guy stirred and rolled over.

"Think we'll be reasonably safe, buddy. Can't be much left in there now, can there?" Chris observed.

Counting agitatedly to five, I blew out a breath and followed his gaze down. "Not a lot, no," I conceded, wearily eyeing my highly polished and sick-spattered shoes.

Oh well, things couldn't get much worse I supposed, pulling out my cell phone as I sloshed toward the men's room.

But they could, of course, I realized, my heart plummeting to about shoe level too. If I hadn't been sure I'd blown it totally with Lisa before, I was now. My pathetic male ego dented, for whatever reason — I wasn't even sure I knew — I'd walked away from the woman I love, leaving her with bewildered tears brimming in her beautiful eyes.

And now I'd lost her.

And I did love her. I think I probably had from the first time I saw her, stuffing her M&S boxes hurriedly in the trash when Becky and I had walked in, and warning her midget JR not to let on that the pre-Christmas dinner was care of Saint Michael.

Lisa had smiled when she saw me; a genuine, dazzling smile that had lit up my world... for a while. How could I not have fallen big time?

I hadn't even told her how I felt. Because I'd been scared she might not have felt the same way? Scared of making a fool of myself? Well — I smiled wryly — I'd managed that last bit competently. Gutted, I dragged a hand through my hair and eyed my mute cell phone. There didn't seem to be much point ringing back. On the basis that actions speak louder, Lisa had made her feelings quite clear. She picked up the call — and then hung up. End of.

"Adam, you amaze me, you really do," I said, my attention on Luke, who was doing his artsy food photography thing with the peaches that were to go into the *Peach Gobbler*.

"Nice to know I'm impressing somebody," Adam said glumly in my ear.

"Utterly amazing." I sighed dreamily as Luke squatted to zoom in on his arrangement at eye level. And builders' butt over his faded jeans, that was not. Bronzed, toned and finger-nail-clutchable, it definitely was.

"Erm, Becks," Adam dragged my thoughts back to him, before they wandered too far, "I'm getting that feeling again. Like, I don't speak the same language as women."

"You don't," I assured him.

"Right." Adam sighed. "Well, I got the message loud and clear when Lisa hung up."

"Well, what do you expect?" I turned my attention to the ingredients for the *Peach Gobbler* before I was tempted to go and sink my teeth into Luke. "She jokily mentions the *M-subject* and you promptly avoid all mention of the subject thereafter. What does this communicate to a woman, do you think, Adam?"

"Erm...?" Adam paused while the cogs went round. "That I think she *is* joking," he tried.

"Adam, are you deliberately being obtuse, or are you really that stupid?"

"The latter," Adam said, after an elongated sigh, "obviously."

"Correct," I answered, careless of his feelings, because Adam had either been careless of Lisa's, or he genuinely was clueless. "Try again, Adam, this time placing yourself in Lisa's shoes."

I waited, one eye on Luke, who was pulling apart a ripe peach with his fingers, fixing me with his Pacific blue, hot-for-sex eyes and... *Mm. Mmm. Mmmm* — I squeezed my eyes closed, then peeled one open and tried not to pant... licking the juice from his fingers. I may have to hang up, if Adam doesn't hurry up, and go and eat Luke wholesale and done with.

"She was embarrassed, wasn't she?" Adam finally had a light bulb moment. "Because she thought I was?"

"*Hallelujah.* Well done, Einstein." I sighed. Then sighed again, my taste buds tingling with anticipated pleasure as Luke walked over, a mischievous smile playing about his mouth and a juicy chunk of peach in his hand. "Enjoy," he said, tempting my salivating mouth with his offering. How could a girl refuse? I allowed him to press the fruit between my lips, and sucked.

"So do you think she might be interested in taking things further then?"

"Adum," I slurped, "she's taken things further. Hold on..." I paused for a necessary lick of lips: Luke's. "She's slept with you. She's allowed Rambo to sleep with you."

Luke paused in his efforts to track a trail of juice down my neck with his tongue.

"Her Jack Russell," I hissed as he surfaced, his curious eyes meeting mine.

Trying not to sound too orgasmic as Luke resumed his gasp-inducing ministrations, I went back to Adam. "She's interested, Adam, trust... *mmm* ...me."

"You think I am in with a chance, then?" Adam sounded distinctly more cheerful.

"Adam," I said trying to keep my voice on an even keel, not easy with a man peppering your clavicle with sizzling hot kisses. "With Lisa, it's a case of love me, love my dog, yes?"

"Uh, huh," Adam agreed, at length. "So?" he added, causing me serious frustration.

"For goodness sake, work it out, Adam," I said, my voice going up several octaves as Luke's luscious lips trailed downwards. "Rambo approves of you. All obstacles to Lisa's heart removed. She's catering for your frickin' mother's golf club do, isn't she? So, how do you *think* she feels about you?"

Adam paused.

I panted, now in imminent danger of abandoning my contributions to, and coordination of, said do, without which poor Lisa would be lost. And Adam's she-witch mom will have won. I very much doubted that the golf club do being a disaster would prove Lisa wasn't good enough for her son. But it would seriously knock Lisa's confidence, and that wasn't on.

"So what should I do?" Adam agonised in one ear, while Luke nibbled erotically on the other. "I've tried to ring... Becky," Adam paused again. I so wished he would hurry up and get on with it, so I could get it on... "Are you okay?"

"Perfect," I mumbled through lips now busy with Luke's.

"You sure? It's just... you sound as if you're being sick."

"Yes, thank you," I replied flatly, my image of me as sensual temptress disappearing into the ether.

"What do I do, Becks?" Adam implored. "I don't want to lose her."

"*Talk* to her." I rolled my eyes, then unable to resist, took a bite of Luke's tongue.

"Talk to her how," Adam asked, sounding now almost as desperate as I felt, "if she won't talk to me?"

God, honestly, do I look like a relationship counsellor? Reluctantly, I dragged my duelling tongue from Luke's. "I don't know, Adam. Drive past her with your blue lights flashing and a big sign flying behind saying 'Idiot on Duty'. Buy shares in Interflora. Get her attention with a romantic gesture. It's not rocket... *Ooh. Mmmm.* Got to go, sorry," I squeaked. "I need to concentrate on my body part. Bready part! For the *Peach Gobbler.* Er, butter's melted. Byee."

"Body part, hmm? Reckon I could help your concentration there," Luke drawled in his seductive Aussie twang, his breath so hot on the back of my neck I almost fell face first into the flour.

"Bready part," I reiterated, flustered. "For the *Peach Gobbler.*" Fanning my flushed face, I attempted to get back into professional cooking mode, before things got too steamy in the kitchen to concentrate on anything but certain parts of Luke's anatomy.

"Ah, right." He nodded, his expression going from uber-suggestive to seriously interested as he turned to the table, which was a total turn on. "Which is?"

Oooh, but the man was growing tastier by the minute. "Like *Peach Cobbler*, to gobble down." Summoning up my will to resist, I diverted my gaze from his tempting lips to the recipe.

"Sounds good," Luke said. "So, where do you want me to start?"

"You mean..." I arched a dubious eyebrow "... you want to help?" Help in the kitchen from my ex was unheard of. In fact, Ryan had been in the vicinity of the kitchen — attempting to wheedle his way back into my life — more times since I'd kicked him out than he had when he lived here.

"Yep." Luke smiled. "On the basis 'many hands make light work'. Then I can get on with the website photography and put my hands to better use after. What d'ythink?"

I think if that's your idea of foreplay, it's working. I offered him a coquettish little smile, rather than myself on a plate, and quietly marveled. Was he for real? "Fab," I said, and decided to put him to the test. "I still have the *Poseidon Serves Up* to make and the *Cheese Cream Ahoi*. And then I have to get it all to the golf club and guide Lisa through the recipes she still has to cook when I get there."

He nodded again. "Okay," he said after a considered second, "no problem. Might as well put me to good use while I'm here, hey?"

"Ooh, I intend to." Smiling appreciatively, I turned to brush his sweet lips with a promissory kiss.

"Butter the 8 x 8 baking dish," I instructed, laughing as his mouth trailed after mine.

"Done." He saluted, two minutes later. "Next, ma'am?"

"Preheat the oven?"

"Mission accomplished," he said, wiping a forearm over his brow, as I gathered the ingredients for the *Cheese Cream Ahoi*. "Next?"

Peach Gobbler

Ingredients for 4 portions:

Bready Part:

1½ cups self-rising flour (OR 1½ cup of regular flour with 2 tsp baking powder)

½ tsp salt

½ cup sugar

1 egg (happy, i.e. organic, and well-beaten beforehand in a small bowl)

½ cup milk

½ cup olive or sunflower oil

Filling:

2 cups of peaches (pitted and cut into slices)

1 dash salt

1 tsp sugar (OR 1 tbsp sugar if you like it sweet)

1 egg (also happy, of course, and also well-beaten beforehand in a small bowl)

Preparation:

Butter an 8 x 8 inch (or thereabouts) baking dish.

Preheat the oven to 200°C.

For the bready part, mix all listed ingredients together in a big bowl. Whisk together until the batter is relatively smooth (it shouldn't be lumpy). It's best to start with the oils, sugar and egg, then add the flour and salt. When it's smooth, set it aside.

Mix the peaches with the salt, sugar and egg in another bowl. All peach pieces should be somewhat coated.

Pour the peach mixture into the greased dish. Pour the bready part over top. Bake for 30 minutes or until the whole top (not just the edges) is golden brown.

Serve warm with vanilla sauce, vanilla ice cream or just as it is.

"I know what I'd like served warm with vanilla ice cream," Luke said with such a soft look of seduction twinkling in his eyes, I melted.

It was no good. The man was just too hard to resist. Puckering up, I'd almost met his lips for a floury kiss when...

"Becky!" came a shout up the hall, the mail slot flapping frantically. "Becky! Answer the door. I need to see you. Now!"

Ooh, frickin' Ryan! Commanding my attention this time. Miffed, and taken aback, I turned toward the hall.

"Uh, uh," Luke said, striding manfully before me. "Hope you don't mind my intervening, Becky, but that bloke is well out of order."

"Not at all. Be my guest," I offered, blinking bemused. Helpful *and* a hero? Good God, he really was a lesser-spotted breed of single, twenty-something gorgeous man.

"This'd better be good, mate," Luke growled, yanking the front door open, unfortunately just as Ryan was squinting through the flap.

"I need to see Becky," Ryan said, to my kneecaps.

Luke assisted him to standing, a little roughly I felt. But then, Ryan had been rather too persistent in his attempts to see me, considering he hardly noticed I existed when he was seeing me. "Whatever you have to say to Becky, you can share with me. Right, Becky?"

I nodded, dumbfounded. I was used to fighting my own battles, but I could get used to this. Which was worrying, because I realized I was falling. And I might just come down to earth with a splat when I found out Luke's interest in me diminished once he'd made good use of his body parts in the bedroom.

"Alone." Ryan met his gaze.

"No dice." Still holding the scruff of his neck, Luke twirled him around. "Sling your hook, mate, and do *not*..."

"It's Lisa!" Ryan choked, halfway out the door.

What? I shook my head. What was he...? "Stop!" I took a step toward him. "Luke, stop."

Luke looked at me, then at Ryan, and did as I asked.

"What about Lisa?" I narrowed my eyes. If Ryan was finding another lame excuse to...

"I tried to ring you," Ryan spluttered, and tugged at his restricting collar.

Luke eyed me again. I nodded. He loosened his hold.

"Your voicemail kept picking up," Ryan said, pulling his offended gaze away from Luke to me.

Because I knew it was him ringing. My tummy turned over. I breathed in, and out, and felt light-headed. "What, Ryan? What about Lisa?"

"I can't be sure," Ryan went on. "I was on the opposite side. They were taking traffic off the motorway and..."

"*What?!*" I screamed. "Ryan, tell me!"

"Lisa's car. I think it was... Lisa's car. There was a little Jack Russell. One of the policemen... I saw him carrying it, and... I tried to ring you, Becky."

"Oh, my God. Oh, my God." I felt Luke's arms around me. I saw Ryan go past me. "Adam," I said, as the floor tilted up to greet me. "Ring Adam. Tell Adam. He'll know what to... oh, dear God."

Not again. Not Lisa. This wasn't happening. This could not be... Jesus... . No!

Panic knotting my stomach, I rammed the passenger door open as my partner skidded to a stop on the hard shoulder.

"*Shit!*" I dragged my hands over my face, squinting against the relentless rain. Fire engines, I noted, fear slicing through my chest. Two of. *Christalmighty,* "No!" Praying uselessly for a miracle, I took off at a run, oblivious to the pain in my ankle and my partner shouting behind me. Slipped. Righted myself, my heartbeat escalating to a steady thud in my chest.

"Adam, wait!" My partner clutched at my jacket. "Wait," he urged me, his eyes locked hard on mine as he faced me. He knew. I know he knew about my wife, about the miracle I'd prayed fervently for then, only for it to go unanswered. I know he wanted to prepare me, to get the heads up before I got to the scene, but there was no way I was going to... what? Stand around and *wait?!*

No way! Scanning my eyes, my partner read what was there. "Go," he said throatily. "But be careful."

"I'm right behind you," he shouted, but I was gone. Mouth dry, heart pounding, hope fading, I banged some illegally-parked idiot driver's door closed, scrambled around the vehicle, and kept going.

Two uniforms, coming toward me. My step faltered. My heart slowed, skipped a beat — and then stopped dead. *Rambo?* I swallowed hard, total panic gripping me now. One of the uniforms was carrying him. The little guy was moving. Was he moving? So where was... she would never leave her dog. Never.

Jesus Christ... "Lisa!?" I shouted, screamed it. My knees buckled. I tried to get past them, needed to get past them.

"Whoa, slow down," one of the uniforms shouted over the roar of traffic from the other side.

"Adam!" My partner caught up behind, caught hold of my shoulders. He said something else. Struggling to break free of his grasp, I couldn't hear him. I didn't want to frickin' well hear him. I needed to...

"She's okay!" Forcing me around to face him, he shook me, literally, until the words registered. "She's okay, Adam. She's..." He relaxed his grip and nodded past me.

Disbelieving, I followed his gaze, and my legs almost gave way. "Lisa?"

"*Rrrrowf?*" went Rambo, pathetically small and hopeful.

Emitting a somewhat strangulated laugh, I closed my eyes and thanked God in earnest, because if ever there was a miracle this had to be it. Trundling to a halt was a motorway patrol car, in the passenger seat of which was the woman I loved and truly thought I'd lost. She was safe. Whether she might want to marry me, have children with me, or just stay friends with me... nothing mattered, other than that she was safe.

Raking a hand shakily through my hair, and cursing my stupid ego which had me walking out on her, I reached carefully for the absolute love of my life, no question. "Hey, small fry," I said as the officer in possession eased Rambo into my arms. "What's with the no attitude, hey?"

In answer to which... yep... "Way to go, Rambo"... he piddled. Poor guy was probably petrified. Loosening my jacket, I tucked him safely inside it, then tuned to limp toward where Lisa was now climbing out of the car.

"Lisa..." I said softly, searching her face as I reached her. If only she knew how much I wanted to pull her into my arms and hold her right then. Hold her like I'd never let go again.

"You're wet," she said, searching mine.

"I know" I smiled, knowing there were tears on my cheeks mingling with incessant rain and not much caring. "You're..."

Beautiful, I didn't get a chance to say, before Lisa squealed, "Rambo, baby!" and peered down my jacket. Rambo wriggled, piddled again probably, but I held on tight.

Trying not to notice the smirks of my colleagues, I waited patiently as, her face all but buried in my chest, she planted a kiss on top of Rambo's head. "Good boy, Rambo," she murmured. "Good little boy. Don't worry. Daddy's got you."

My partner arched an eye. So did I. Had I just been promoted?

"Thank you," Lisa said, finally blinking up at me, bedraggled but definitely beautiful.

I furrowed my brow. "For what?" I hadn't actually done anything.

"Riding to my rescue." She smiled her dazzling smile.

"I'd swim an ocean for you, Lisa." I swallowed, and wished our audience would give us some space.

Lisa studied me curiously, her head cocked to one side.

Wondering what kind of man it was who would throw a tantrum while she was catering for his mother's frickin' golf club do, I supposed. I needed to try and put that right. To apologize now, whoever was looking on. "Lisa, I'm..." I started.

Then stopped, as Lisa stood up on tiptoe to plant a soft kiss on my lips, which felt pretty good. Rambo's tongue, however…

Lisa laughed and dropped back down in deference to her dog. "I think Rambo loves you," she said.

"Yeah." I laughed, wishing I had the guts to ask if there was a chance his mistress might too. "Ditto," I said awkwardly, then wrapped an arm around her and pulled her close.

Chapter 10 The Course of True Love

True love never did run smooth. Four courses to go — minus the *Pizza Cookie* and *Jammed in There* — and the clock was ticking

I could see why Demi Moore got so frustrated with Patrick Swayze in Ghost. Similarly frustrated and confused as to Adam's true feelings for me, I pondered his answer to my soul-baring statement while perusing the ingredients for the *Pizza Cookie* (the huge cookie baked on a pizza sheet and delectable — according to the recipe). I'd doubted it would be very delectable without the essential chocolate chips and chopped nuts though, thus my frantic trip into town to purchase essentials. A trip too far for my run-down PT Cruiser it turned out, which — at 80mph, ahem — had coughed and spluttered, emitted a plume of acrid black smoke and then committed suicide on the motorway.

"I mean, what kind of answer is 'Ditto' when one declares one's love to someone, hey, sweetie?" I addressed my midget JR in the absence of any other available audience.

"*Grrrowf.*" Recovered from his ordeal — a mad scramble down the embankment lest he get singed or squished — he was now right by my side, possibly hoping I'd drop a few chocolate chips, Rambo gave his squeaky piggy a rattling good shake.

"Precisely," I agreed, miffed at Adam's apparent inability to grasp the obvious. Okay, admittedly, I'd said Rambo was in love with him, but you'd think he'd have got the hint.

Squeeak. Rambo obviously agreed.

Perhaps if I went out and drew on the sooty hood of my car? I peered huffily out of the kitchen window, beyond which Adam was peering under said hood alongside the road assistance man, much 'tsk'ing and shaking of heads going on, from which I gleaned the man-that-can couldn't fix it. My poor cremated car had obviously gone to the great breakers in the sky. Which begged the question, how on earth was I supposed to transport the *Faith in Salad, Green Soup, Drunken Chicken*, Adam's *Olivia's Pride* and the *Pizza Cookie* to the golf club for… I glanced at the clock, and almost swallowed my tonsils. "*Eeek!*" I was supposed be there in an *hour?! Hell.* I chewed worriedly on my lip.

Squeeak. Squeeak. Rambo chomped frantically on Piggy.

One hour? Sixty miniscule little minutes to produce a whole menu *and* reinvent myself as a confident hostess with the mostest? I couldn't do it. I'd need more than a makeover; I'd need a freaking miracle. My hair wasn't just frizzy it was frizzled. No amount of serum was going to fix burnt ends. As for my make-up? I dashed to the hall mirror to survey the damage. "Oh, my... God."

"Yes, my child?" Adam said wittily, as he came through the front door.

I scowled, then quickly straightened my face, lest he think he'd inadvertently wandered onto a horror set.

"You okay?" he said softly behind me.

"No." I blinked forlornly at my zombie-ish complexion. "I think I might have died."

Adam's semi-amused expression quickly changed to one of concern. "Come on," he said, wrapping a comforting arm around my shoulders. I so wanted to turn around, bury my face in his chest and stay there forever, "you need to lie down. I'll ring my mom and tell her to find some other idiot..."

"I'm not an idiot!" I bristled, indignant.

"Lisa I didn't mean..." Adam trailed off wearily, probably wondering how he came to be involved with a demented-haired woman, and how he could discreetly extract himself a.s.a.p. "You're a lovely, kind person, Lisa, but you've done enough for this silly catering do, and almost killed yourself doing it. Mom can get her golf club cronies to pick up the stuff we've already cooked and serve it up herself. Meanwhile, bed for you, madam."

Ooh, yeah. I went a bit limp at the thought. Alas, much as I would quite like to have dragged Adam upstairs and instructed him to keep his hat on, I couldn't. I'd come this far and I was damned if I was going to have Her Maj looking snootily down her nose at me, reminding me I didn't measure up to his perfect wife — God rest her — for evermore. That's if Adam wanted to be with me anymore, if he did have any feelings for me beyond fondness. He had that, I was sure.

"No," I said, stoically hoisting up my shoulders. "I've promised to do it, and it's too late to back out now. Your mom's still on crutches, Adam, remember?"

"As if she'd let me forget." Adam dragged a hand over his neck. "It wouldn't be fair to let her down now."

In any case, I was the new me, I'd decided. Not clingy or needy, looking for commitment or any of those unattractive things that would have a man running a mile. Sassy, independent, confident, fun and carefree, that was me. I headed gloomily for the kitchen, wondering if a Brillo Pad updo would suit my new image, and whether I could confidently whip up a *Pizza Cookie* in three seconds flat.

"Okay, okay." Adam sighed, limping in behind me. "You're a braver man than I am. I'll give you a hand."

Man? I wasn't sure whether to be flattered or offended. Is that what I was in his eyes, a friend? *Humph.* Attempting to get his somewhat distracted attention, I flicked back my frizz and puffed out my debatable cleavage.

"So what are we cooking?" Adam asked, oblivious to my subtle display of feminine wiles.

Offended, definitely, but that was okay; I was sassy and independent and... stuff. I deflated a bit. "*Pizza Cookie.* The *Stack O' Cakes...*" which was on his menu list and which he hadn't done, I didn't mention, being the new carefree me, "...and *Frisian Anchor* I'm going to do in situ," I informed him, oozing confidence. *Help.*

"Right, well, I'll help out here, get my partner to drop you off at the club, check in at the station and then meet you at the designated time with Becky and the rest of the dishes. Sound like a plan?"

"Perfect." I nodded and waited, hoping Adam might suggest something nice but naughty for dessert.

"Do you want me to cook or pass stuff?" he asked.

My shoulders drooped. "Um, pass stuff," I said, swallowing back a little lump in my throat. "And read the instructions, if you would, but fast."

Adam glanced curiously at me.

"I still have to make myself gorgeous." I glanced at him, hoping he might give me one of his bone-melting smiles and tell me I was. He didn't. *Right. Fine. Needy? Not me.* "You know," I went on airily, "being a *wo*man."

"Ah, right." He nodded, clueless. "You'll need some time, then?"

"Obviously," I said, with a merry little chuckle, and tried very hard to hang on to my plummeting ego.

"Lisa, can I ask you something?"

"Of course," I said, my ego bobbing eagerly back to the surface. "Anything." Was this it? He'd obviously been deep in thought. Pondering things possibly? Was he about to pick up the conversation around the scary four-letter word?

"What were you doing exactly, when your car caught fire?"

Oh. Apparently not. "Um, nothing." I tried not to mind. "I just popped a CD in and... *whoosh*... my dashboard caught fire."

"Something hot, was it? The CD?" Adam asked, jokily.

"*Beyonce*," I said, reaching for the recipe.

"Wow, red hot then?" He waggled his eyebrows.

And my ego disappeared without trace.

"Erm, joking, Lisa," he said, as I passed him the recipe, eyes averted, lest they shoot red-hot daggers into his.

"Hilarious, I am sure." I smiled flatly. "Shall we get on, so I can go upstairs and perform major body surgery?"

Adam squinted at me, puzzled. "Erm, right," he said, dragging his hand over his neck. "So, here we go."

"Ooh, slow down," I said when he got to the cream cheese, scrambling around the working surface.

"You said you wanted fast."

"Not that fast." I didn't look at him, because he was starting to sound stressed, and if we were about to argue, again, I was sure my waning confidence would fly straight out of the window.

Adam paused after the ingredients and waited. "Are you with me?"

Good question. "Um, ahem, possibly, yes."

"Right, okay, so here come the baking instructions."

Pizza Cookie

Ingredients for 2 12-inch cookies:

1 cup olive oil

¾ cup white sugar

¾ cup brown sugar (packed)

1 cup cream cheese

1 tsp vanilla extract

2 eggs (happy!)

2¼ cups self-rising flour (OR 2¼ cups of regular flour with 1 tsp baking soda)

1 pinch salt

1½ cups chocolate chips

1 cup chopped nuts (or seeds if you are allergic to nuts. You could also leave these out entirely)

Baking Instructions:

Preheat your oven to 180°C and lightly grease two 12-inch pizza pans. If you don't have more than one pan, no problem, just bake one cookie first and after that one has cooled, bake the second.

Using a whisk, mix the white and brown sugars, cream cheese, vanilla and eggs together in a big bowl. In a second bowl, mix the flour, salt and baking soda together with a fork.

Add the flour mixture to the sugar mixture one spoon at a time, working it in before adding more (if you add all the flour together at the same time it will get lumpy and be hard to smooth out). When the mixture is smooth and creamy-looking, add the chocolate chips and nuts, mixing together.

Divide the dough in half and spread each half evenly in its own pan.

Bake for about 25 minutes, or until the top is golden brown.

Take out of the oven, but leave the cookies in the pan; just cool them completely on wire racks. When the cookies are totally cool, they will be solid enough to cut into slices.

Serve by itself or as a side/main dessert with something else, such as vanilla ice cream.

"How's it going?" Adam peered into my bowl, me still being at the 'trying to get the mixture smooth and creamy-looking' stage.

"Lumpily," I admitted miserably.

Adam didn't say anything for a second, then, "That'll be because you..."

"Added more than one spoonful at a time, I know!" I banged the spoon down, and splotched myself in the eye. Wonderful. Now, I looked like a one-eyed zombie.

Adam shook his head, obviously taken aback. "Lisa..." he started, but previous relationship issues — his and mine — to the fore, I was in no mood to listen.

"I'm trying, Adam, I really am," I said tearfully. "I can't help it if I'm not as perfect as Melissa. If my living room paper was only good enough for her toilet. If I'm not as competent as her in the kitchen. As competent as you. I'm not even sure I want to be!"

"Jesus, Lisa..." Adam laughed, incredulously. "I don't frickin'..."

"Lisa! Sweetie!" We both whirled around as Becky — obviously having let herself in with the spare key — bowled into the kitchen, face stricken, arms outstretched. "Oh, God, I thought you were dead!"

Pausing briefly...

"Grrrrr. Rrrrrowf!

... when she stepped on Piggy, Becky flew across the kitchen to pull me to her abundant bosom.

Safe in my best friend's embrace, and not caring that I might look clingy or needy, I squeezed my eyes closed. "I almost wish I was," I whispered to her clavicle.

"Oh, hon..." She bravely smoothed down my Brillo Pad. "Poor you! It must have been dreadful. Adam said you were coping, but you're obviously not, so why on earth are you doing all..."

"I *am* coping." I sniffled back my tears, and debated whether I could wear Becky as a face-saving accessory. "I was, but..."

Becky lifted my chin, scrutinized my telltale eyes, and then turned angrily on Adam. "It obviously is rocket science, isn't it?" she growled, giving him a sub-zero glare. "What has he done, hon?" She turned back to me, blinking her eyelash extensions sympathetically.

"Nothing," I lied, because he hadn't, not really. "It's just... I feel a bit wobbly, that's all."

"*Humph.*" Becky wasn't convinced. She turned back to Adam. "Well?"

"Nothing," he echoed me, hands splayed helplessly. "I said Lisa should lie down. I told her not to do this," he went on, sounding exasperated now.

Becky continued to glare at him.

"It's shock probably," Adam said, less stridently. "Delayed shock. Bound to be after the accident."

"Preceded by the argument." Becky added pointedly.

Adam dropped his gaze.

"And in order to assist, you did...?"

"Nothing." Adam mumbled to his shoes.

"No flowers?"

Adam raked his hand though his hair.

"A dandelion out of the garden possibly?" Becky snapped. "God, honestly! Well done, Adam. Go to the top of the class. Why don't you just step on her dog now and be done with it?! Come on, sweetie."

Me in hand, Becky twirled around to huff back across the kitchen, narrowly missing Rambo in favor of Piggy...

"*Grrrrrrrr.*"

...again, ejecting a squeaky from his mouth, and giving me cause to ponder where the previously ejected squeak might be.

"Let's go up and get you good and gorgeous," she said, leading me onward.

"As long as you have a handy plastic surgeon in tow." I sighed dejectedly. Then gawped interestedly, as a Greek God appeared in my hall.

"G'day." He smiled, sunlight-pinging off his ultra-white teeth.

Correction: Australian. The food-photographer, I gathered, and, "Ooh, yum," I couldn't help myself, "now he *is* red-hot."

Yeah, well, Lisa might think he was hot stuff, but Rambo had other ideas.

"Grrr*owwwf. Rrrowwwf. Grrrrrr.*"

Atta boy. I tried not to smirk as the little guy went from cutie to Rottie, front legs bouncing off the floor, then panting around in a circle, determined to see the intruder off with killer bite to the ankle.

"Hiya, mate." The guy parked his camera on the table and bent to pick him up.

"Erm…" I wouldn't if I were you, I was going to say, but to be honest, the fact that Lisa had obviously noted he was a walking surfboarding advert, no doubt with waxed and toned chest to complete the image, had royally pee'd me off.

Whoops, too late. "He gets a bit nervous," I imparted, as the guy looked equally pee'd off. Or rather pee'd on.

"Leaks a bit, doesn't he?" the guy observed, holding Rambo at arms-length.

"A lot," I assured him, taking Rambo off him. Rambo's hind legs dangled like chicken legs, and his 'leaky bit' was pointed straight at me. He couldn't help piddling when he was nervous, I knew, but I was praying he didn't right then, preferring to be seen as someone he was used to being around. Not that I would be much now I'd screwed things up again, I supposed.

I'd wanted to tell Lisa I loved her, that I was sorry for the stupid misunderstanding around the marriage subject — to bring her flowers. But stopping by the florists on the way to an accident she was involved in, not knowing whether she was… it didn't seem high on the agenda somehow. And squeezing a life-changing statement in between the vanilla extract and the nuts while talking fast wasn't going to work, was it? I couldn't get my head around why Lisa thought I wanted her to be like Melissa though. I'd loved my wife, but that was then and this was now, and I loved Lisa because she was who *she* was. If only I could ever find the right time to tell her.

"Luke," the guy introduced himself, extending his hand.

I hoisted Rambo up, attempting to tuck him in the crook of my arm, at which point Rambo attempted a French kiss, seriously damaging my macho image. "Adam." I offered my hand, trying to look unfazed, like I was used to such displays of open affection. "Lisa's, erm...?"

"Bloke, I know."

Glad somebody did.

"I'm Becky's food photographer, and hoping-to-be bloke. Guess that depends on how this golf club thing goes. It's got her really stressed out, you know?"

"Tell me about it." I sighed. Looked like we were both in the same boat. Maybe I didn't need to train Rambo to pee on his camera after all.

"So I've offered to help out," Luke said, setting up his tripod, "though I'm more into photographing food than cooking it, to be honest."

I managed a smile. "Ditto."

"Stressed out about her mate, she was, too. Glad she's okay, by the way."

"She had a narrow escape." I sucked in a breath, winded by a sudden flashback of someone who hadn't.

Luke obviously caught my expression. "You care about her, don't you?"

"And then some," I admitted, wondering when it was I started doing guy talk.

"Just a suggestion, but maybe you should tell her. She looked pretty wracked coming into the hall just now."

Like I hadn't thought of that, or already had the speech from... uh, oh, talk of the devil.

Becky appeared at the door, looking also 'wracked'. "A word, if I may, Adam?"

In private I assumed, as she wasn't coming in, probably because she didn't want 'hopeful' to hear her give me an earful. "Come on, small-fry," I said, holding onto Rambo on the basis that she wouldn't wallop a guy with an innocent dog in his arms.

"*Talk* to her!" Becky hissed, once I was in earshot.

Here we go, again. I rolled my eyes.

"Don't look like that." She definitely looked close to clobbering me now.

"Well, how do you expect me to look?" I asked, exasperated. "I know I need to talk to her. I'm trying, ferchrissakes. I might have if you..."

"She's really upset."

"Yeah." I smiled wryly. "She didn't sound that upset when she clocked your 'hoping-to-be guy'."

"I don't frickin' believe this." Becky laughed, incredulous. "Don't worry, Adam," she gave me a look, which translated into *idiot*. "Luke prefers *Beyonce* types."

With which she flounced into the kitchen, leaving me wondering how big a hole it was I had to dig myself out of.

My hoping-to-be bloke? *Hmm?* I eyed Luke interestedly, as Adam took his leave with Lisa. And if he didn't talk to her, properly, before the night was out, he'd be taking his leave, period. I hope he'd got that message loud and clear.

Luke, it seemed, intended to stick around — and we hadn't even got to the body parts bit yet. *Ummm, mmm. Tempt-a-licious.*

I ran my tongue over my lips and my eyes over him as I finished up Lisa's *Pizza Cookie*, which I managed to smooth into the pan despite it being a bit lumpy. Luke definitely had a way with fruit, artistically arranging an apple and pear around the *Jammed in There*. He'd already taken a few shots, but didn't think they were aesthetically pleasing enough, the marmalade having been pre-prepared and already jarred.

"So what else goes in there?" he asked, stepping back and clicking his camera.

He was genuinely interested. And I was fast becoming smitten. Ryan and I had parted friends, just on the basis that he cared enough to dash over to tell me about Lisa's terrible accident — and collect his missing CDs while he was there — but Luke *really* cared about me, about what I cared about. Maybe this golf club thing wasn't going to be such a disaster after all?

"Pumpkin," I laughed, imagining what he might do with that. "But Lisa doesn't have one of those handy in her fruit bowl."

"Pity." He turned around to give me a sex-loaded smile and take a quick snap of me — au natural, as he preferred me to be, apparently.

Sigh. I lingered over an image of Luke au natural and tried not to pant. "And?" he asked, maintaining his interest — and mine. I may have to give in to temptation and ravage him on Lisa's kitchen table in a minute.

Oh. Maybe not. My eyes fell on Rambo, sitting mouse-like under the table. A dog he might be, but he still looked all-seeing and knowing to me.

"The recipe's in my bag," I said, "if you really want to know."

"Absolutely. Helps with the composition," Luke said, leaning across the table to replace Lisa's fruit in her bowl.

Stretched denim over firm buttocks. *Slurrrrp.* I turned to fetch the recipe, giving my face a quick fan with it before I handed it to him. "There you go. It seems complicated, but it's actually easy."

I watched while he read. God, his eyelashes were gorgeous.

"Sounds good. How about we have some for breakfast?" Luke turned his gaze on mine, his dreamy blue eyes hopeful, yet smouldering with sexual innuendo.

Ooh, be still my rampaging libido. "You're staying for breakfast then?" I asked, all nonchalance, lest he glean I'd been contemplating chaining him to the bedpost and asking the vicar to do a house call.

"As long as you'll have me," he said, his gaze straying to my lips.

Oh, I will, honey. In every conceivable way.

Close your eyes, Rambo.

Jammed in There

Ingredients for 6-8 glasses:

4 pounds mixed fruit and vegetables: pumpkin, apple, and pear

1 cup water

1 tsp ginger or cinnamon

3 cups sugar

1 lemon, including the zest

Preparation:

Cut the fruit and vegetables and remove the pits, stones and seeds. Cook the pieces in the water until they are soft.

Place a fine sieve over a second pot and push the fruit mash through this sieve with a cooking spoon to remove all peel and most of the pulp. This will give the jam a much more pleasant texture and cooking the peel along with the fruit is important for the flavor.

When all fruit has been sieved, add the lemon zest, juice and ginger (or cinnamon, if you don't like ginger).

Cook this until it thickens (this can take up to an hour, depending on the apple). Every now and then you will want to stir, so don't walk too far away, otherwise it might burn. To find out if the jam is thick enough, spread a little bit of it on a cold plate. If it jells up, it's right. Otherwise, give it a few more minutes and repeat the jell test.

Now, place your clean jam jars in the sink and pour boiling water over and into them and the lids. Take them out, removing all water and pour the jam into the hot jars. Close them, remove any spills, and place them upside down on the counter. After about 10 minutes, turn them back around (this will seal them).

Chapter 11 Food for Thought

He wasn't saying much. I eyed Adam sideways as we sped toward the golf club. But then, he couldn't really, I supposed, with his partner at the wheel. Equally, he couldn't be very physically effusive with said partner looking on and a bowl of *Green Soup* perched on his lap. I prayed we wouldn't hit any bumps, while debating whether Adam would notice if I lifted the lid of the tureen and had a quick peek inside.

No, the new not-quite-so-confident-as-I'd-like-to-be me, decided. Rambo's missing squeaky couldn't possibly have plopped in the pot. One dropping in there had been bad luck, especially with Her Maj peering through my kitchen window when it landed, but a second floating atop the Gazpacho? Impossible. About as likely as me winning the lottery.

"Okay?" Adam caught my hand as my fingers tiptoed casually across the seat.

Oooh! "Oops, yes," I assured him, flushing guiltily. "You took me by surprise, that's all."

"You don't mind my taking you... *ahem*... your hand, then?" He glanced at me, a flicker of uncertainty in his delicious, chocolaty brown eyes — and my heart bobbed up from where it had been wallowing miserably in self-pity.

Mind? Mind? He could take me, body and soul, right here on the back seat — if his partner would be so kind as to close his eyes. "No. Take away," I said happily, sliding my hand more comfortably into his — and wishing I had the foresight to bring a tube of superglue.

He might think bouncy *Beyonce* was 'red-hot' compared to flat little me, but he did still fancy me, didn't he? And if he didn't love me, in the all-consuming way lovers do, he did love me a little, didn't he?

"Good." Adam squeezed my hand.

"Make mine a chicken balti," his partner quipped from the front, eyes obviously wide open and spoiling the mood a bit. "With a stuffed Keema Nan."

"Fun-ny." Adam rolled his eyes. "Not. Keep your eyes on the road, James, yes?"

"Yes sir. Sorry sir." His partner mock-saluted. "Would sir like me to close the privacy grill?"

"Your mouth, James. That would be good."

"*Mmmmf. Mmmmf,*" was the muffled response.

I laughed. I couldn't help it. I was glad Adam worked with someone nice.

"Witty, isn't he?" Adam's mouth twitched into a smile, which suited him much better than the broody look he'd been wearing since we left.

I wished we hadn't argued, that the heavy subject of marriage hadn't popped up, making things awkward between us. That first night — our only night — of tender lovemaking together had been so special, so different for me. We'd been so comfortable together, easy banter passing between us over Rambo's head and Adam's balding parrot squawking, '*Who's a clever boy then?*'

I liked him much more smiley. I liked *him*; that was important in my mind if love was to survive. He made *me* smile. He'd saved my little Jack Russell's life, limping and in pain, practically throwing himself in front of an oncoming car. His horrible she-witch mother aside, Adam was nice, right down to the core. I knew it. I felt it. I so hoped his broody contemplation wasn't because he didn't feel the same way, and didn't know how to tell me now we'd both been sucked into this golf club catering fiasco.

"We are meeting up, aren't we?" Adam glanced quickly toward his partner, obviously not wanting to get too personal, which really would be difficult in the back of a patrol car with a bowl of *Green Soup* between us. "After the do, I mean?"

"Yes, of course," I said, then toned down my eagerness in case he did think I'd been wistfully selecting my wedding dress when I'd joked Rambo was. "That's if you want to."

He nodded thoughtfully. "We need to talk," he said, giving my hand another squeeze — and my tummy flipped over.

Talk? Oh, God. Quelling a sudden queasiness, I turned to gaze out of the side-window as we turned onto the highway. It was only two junctions, the quickest route to the club, but too long to be holding his hand without connecting emotionally. There was so much I wanted to say, yet had no words. No opportunity. What would he say... when we talked?

I could feel Adam stealing glances at me, but I kept my eyes fixed sideways, noting the spot where I'd pulled up on the hard shoulder, quite sure I was going to be frizzled as well as frazzled. And then ran for my life, Rambo in arms, scrambling down the embankment as smoke erupted from my car like from a volcano. Where Adam had searched for me, terror in his eyes, tears on his cheek when he'd found me.

He *must* care about me, mustn't he?

Adam tightened his grip on my hand.

He did. Tentatively I squeezed his hand back, and...

"Ouch!"

...Adam almost stopped my circulation.

"*Hell*, sorry." He quickly loosened his hold. "I wasn't thinking. Was thinking. I... we need to talk, Lisa," he said, his eyes meeting mine as I turned.

Eyes where dark shadows danced, I noticed.

A chill ran through me.

"Can we, do you think, honestly?" Adam glanced down and then nervously back — and a little piece of me curled up and died.

Gulping back my trepidation, I smiled and nodded, not sure what else to do.

Okay, so I might not be very fun and carefree when I heard what he needed to say, urgently obviously, but I could be... well, just me, someone caring — I tugged up my shoulders — because sassy and independent I might not be, but that's what I sensed he might need me to be.

Oh, my God! I un-suckered my lips from Luke's as my eye caught the clock, then retracted my nails from his back so fast I almost skinned him.

"What's the emergency?" Luke asked rearranging his shirt over his firm torso, causing me another hot flush.

"The *Cheese Cream Ahoi*! I haven't made it! And there's still the *Poseidon Serves Up* to do. Where *does* the time go?"

"When you're having fun?" Luke tacked on.

"Definitely," I assured him, my eyes lingering hungrily behind me as I skidded to the sink. "I'll have to cook the fish dish while I'm instructing Lisa on the *Frisian Anchor*, I suppose. Do you think she'll have her hands-free?"

I gave my hands a rinse and dashed back to the working surface.

"Dunno," Luke said, retrieving his camera and flashing me the *Pizza Cookie* photos, which had turned out pretty well considering he'd been distracted. He was good. *Mmmm.* Most definitely.

Down girl. I averted my eyes from temptation before he seduced me away from the cooking again. This golf club thing was important to Lisa. And getting the photography bit right was important to me — and to Luke, who was obviously an artist, ergo would be bound to build me a stunning website for my new catering business, which I was uber-excited about. I'd even tentatively thought up a name, *Food for Thought*, which I hoped might sound upmarkety enough to pique interest.

"I reckon her guy would quite like her to have her hands-free though," Luke went on.

"So she can tend to his needs once she finished catering for his cow of a mother, you mean?" I gave him a look as I flew around the kitchen, selecting ingredients: *Camembert, butter, cream cheese...*

"So he can *talk* to her," Luke elucidated, with a tolerant smile.

"Talk? Adam?" I laughed, incredulously. "He'll need an instruction manual to do that. The man's absolutely hopeless."

"Maybe." Luke shrugged, then...

"Grrr*rrr*."

... skirted carefully around Rambo, who was guarding his squeakless piggy toy from further assault. "He cares about her though, trust me."

"I'm sure he does, but a girl needs to hear the magic words, Luke."

"What? I love you?"

Oh, wow! It came out *I lav you* in his soft Aussie accent, but *sooo* sexy, it would make some lucky girl orgasmic one day. "Precisely," I said lightly, though my heart suddenly felt like lead.

Which was silly. It wasn't like either of us were expecting anything more than a brief encounter, preferably with lots of steamy hot sex. I was okay with that. I was a self-sufficient, grown woman and quite capable of handling a fulfilling sexual relationship with no strings attached.

Luke was just passing through, and I didn't mind that, not a bit. He'd already eased my broken-relationship blues, provided a beautiful distraction. And he was beautiful. I glanced at him over my shoulder, my eyes travelling from his sun-kissed hair to his glute-accentuating jeans, taking in his sculpted chest and taut stomach en route. God but he was. Utterly *yummy*. I sighed longingly. But — I gave myself a reality check — while I had the boobs, I doubted I'd measure up to the Baywatch sort he'd normally frolic with, no doubt fall in love with, and marry.

I was fine with it though. I'd gone into this with my eyes open. So, why did I feel a sense of bereavement I hadn't felt when Ryan and I split?

"Right, well," Luke coughed behind me, "here's hoping they work some magic then, because I reckon I probably do."

Sh...ugar!! I squeezed my eyes closed. "Sorry?" I said, my voice rather high-pitched.

"I love you," Luke whispered so close to my ear, I squashed my Camembert.

"*What?!*" I whirled around, my heart soaring so high it almost leapt right out of my mouth.

"I said," Luke brushed my forehead with his lips, "I..." my nose "love..." my lips "... you." He finished with such a warm twinkle in his eye I almost cried.

"Oh, God," I sniffled instead, and dragged a splotch of ripe Camembert under my nose.

"I love your *Cassata Seduction*. I love your *Jammed in There*. I love your hair, your smile, your style." He paused, while I gawped. "I love you."

Was he serious? I searched his face, utterly flabbergasted.

Luke looked a little awkward, then, "Do you think you might... you know?" He shrugged hopefully.

I stared at him, then *ooooh*, "Yessss!" Giddy with pleasure, I shrieked so loud Rambo almost jumped out of his fur.

"Yes, Yesss, Yessss!" Throwing myself at Luke, I locked my arms around his neck.

Rrrowf. Rrrrowwff. Rambo's ears pricked up. His stumpy tail shot up. He plucked up his piggy and shook it excitedly around in a circle.

"I take it that's a yes?" Luke mumbled, as I went for a full frontal assault on his tonsils.

"Uh, huh." I confirmed breathlessly. "Absolutely."

"In which case," Luke said, squeezing my bottom, "we'd better..." nibbling my tongue "... get these recipes sorted, so we can, er...?"

"I suppose," I sighed, "though I am *soooo* tempted to drag you bodily into the bedroom..."

"In which case, we'd better get these recipes sorted pronto." He smiled his delicious, sex-loaded smile. "Come on, the world's depending on you."

Well, Lisa was, I reminded myself. And she did mean the world to me. "Okay, onward." I reluctantly extracted myself from Luke's arms.

"*Cheese Cream Ahoi*," I said, glancing around for my recipe.

"The menu." Luke found it. He looked at me, his eyes coming to rest on my lips.

I looked at him.

Tongues met.

"Ahem." Luke eased himself away, before I digested him.

"You taste great, too," Luke commented, as I tripled up on the ingredients, six people have chosen this for starters, apparently.

"I do?" I preened inwardly, feeling like a sexual Goddess.

"Yup." Luke assured me. "Ripe Camembert is probably an acquired taste but it does it for me."

"Thank you." I hit him, but not too hard, lest I damage the delectable goods.

"I love it when you're rough with me." Luke smirked and read on.

"Taste?" I offered Luke a lick of my fork.

"Exquisite." He licked his lips.

I licked his lips. "Mmm, divine."

Cheese Cream Ahoi

Ingredients for 2-4 portions:
1 cup Camembert (very ripe)
1 tbsp butter
½ cup cream cheese
1 onion (chopped as finely as possible)
Salt, pepper
Paprika powder
3 tbsp beer
Onion rings and chives for garnish
6-8 chicory leaves

Take the Camembert out of the fridge the day before you want to prepare the cheese cream.

On the next day, crush the Camembert with a fork.

Mix the butter, cream cheese, beer, and chopped onion in with the cheese and spice with salt, pepper and paprika powder to taste. Do be careful to not sample too much as it is delicious.

Let sit for about one hour. Spread the cheese cream on individual chicory leaves for a buffet.

This tastes great on dark bread or with fresh pretzels, garnished with onion rings and chives.

Serve a wheat beer alongside, or any other beer you and your loved one prefer.

"Beez Neez," said Luke.

"Definitely," I agreed, my lips wandering back in search of his.

"No, Becky, I mean the beer. It's an Australian honey wheat..."

"Nectar." I sighed. "*Slurrr... Pffft.*" Blowing out another sigh, I unpuckered my lips as my cell phone rang, rudely interrupting my playtime.

"OhmiGosh, Lisa!" Noting her number, I grabbed up the phone and flapped a hand toward my *Poseidon Serves Up* recipe.

Luke dutifully obliged and turned to fetch it. Bless his... lovely firm buttocks. *Stop it.* I dragged my attention away from the gorgeous view, back to Lisa.

"We're here," she hissed in my ear.

"Right, okay, hon." I got into business mode. "I'm right there beside you," I assured her.

"No you're not. You're there." Lisa sounded distinctly wobbly. "I don't think I can do this, Becks."

"Of course you can. You have your hands-free. I'll be right alongside you every step of the way, and when I get there I'll help you serve up. Everything's going to be..."

"But that's the trouble, the... *crackle*... and... *crackle, crackle*... she'll guess. I just know she..."

"Lisa, I can't hear a word you're saying. Why are you whispering?"

"Because we're late," Lisa whispered.

"Oh. Right." I rolled my eyes, offered Luke an apologetic smile, and scanned the ingredients list he was holding considerately for my perusal.

Poseidon Serves Up

Ingredients for 6 portions:

2 pounds fish (fillet is best)

½ cup breadcrumbs

1½ tsp each salt and pepper

¼ tsp curry

½ cup cream

½ cup butter

For the sauce:

3 tbsp butter (melted)

3 peppers (one green, one red, one yellow)

2 cups prawns

1 onion

1 tbsp salt

1 cup cream

1 cup cream cheese

1 cup rice

pinch of turmeric

Cut the fish into bite-sized chunks. Mix the curry with the cream in a bowl.
Mix breadcrumbs with salt and pepper and put this in a big deep plate.
Cover the fish pieces in the curry cream first, then in breadcrumbs. Fry the fish in butter for 2 minutes per side and place in a greased oven-proof dish.
Cut the onion and peppers into small dice and braise in butter.
Mix the ingredients for the sauce in a bowl and cover the fish in this.
Bake everything in the oven for about 15 minutes.
Rice tastes good with this dish. To make rice, take 1 cup of rice for 3 people, and cover this with 2 cups of water. Bring to a rapid boil, turn off the heat and leave on the burner with the lid on — the rice will just get ready all by itself. For this very dish, add some turmeric to the rice for color.

"Brill. Thanks," I mouthed, loving the man more by the second as he walked back across the kitchen to check that the *Cheese Cream Ahoi* was saran-wrapped and ready to go, along with the dark bread, pretzels, onion rings and chives.

Lisa's whispers, meanwhile, were becoming more frantic by the second. "Her Maj is coming out to greet us and she's looking at us as if she's encountered a bad smell, and the car plopped down a pothole, and..."

"Whoa, Lisa; deep breaths, sweetie. Seven in... come on, breathe with me... nine out. Seven in..."

"Better?"

"Mm," Lisa said in a little voice.

Not, obviously. "Where's Adam?" I asked, going over to the working surface to get started on the baked fish dish a bit quickish. Lisa, I suspected, might just be on the verge of hyperventilating and dying, which wouldn't go down terribly well at the she-witch mother's posh golf club do.

"Bringing the *Drunken Chicken* from the car. And it's raining and his uniform's green and... oh, God, it's sticking out!"

"Pardon?"

"My hands-free thingy. It's protruding. She's bound to..."

"Put Adam on the line," I said, without further ado.

"I can't. Her Maj is making cross faces at him. Oh, Becky. It's a disaster. Already. He looks absolutely miserable."

Not half as miserable as he'll be when I get there. I growled inwardly. "Lisa, go on in. Get things set up. I'll talk you through the dishes you still have to prepare, and I'll be with you a.s.a.p., if not sooner."

Sensing trouble, Luke had started on the menu by the time I ended the call. "I'm guessing you could use a hand?" he said, selecting a fillet of fish.

"Two." I sighed, wearily this time, and passed him the knife

"So let me give it a go while you get yourself sorted. And don't worry," he gave me a slow wink, "I'm worth waiting for."

Yes — I passed him the cooking instructions, but the question was, could I?

Shivering outside the golf club, I waited while Her Maj walked haughtily past me to have a 'brief word with her son'. A derogatory word, no doubt. Why on earth Adam put up with her, I really didn't know. Except he was her son, of course. And the alternative was to walk away.

Cocking the ear my protuberance wasn't wedged in, I had a good listen. God, she really was awful. It was a wonder she wasn't using a broomstick for a crutch.

"Adam, your uniform!" She looked him up and down, aghast. "You look an absolute disgrace. And you're limping! This really is too much, Adam, running around after Lucy..."

"Lisa!" Adam cut in, angrily. "Her *name* is Lisa. Get it right, Mom," he lowered his tone, glancing in my direction, "or we're gone, end of."

Hah! I could see Isabelle's mouth dropping open even from six yards away. She looked like a startled guppy. Served her right, silly old trout. I'd have been tempted to kick her crutch from under her.

"*Mon Dieu!*" Isabelle clutched a hand to her chest, horrified. "Really, Adam... is this the way you talk to your poor Maman, after she's done her best for you, given birth to you, brought you up practically single-handedly. Scrimped and saved...?"

"And there lies the problem, doesn't it, Mom?" Adam stopped her before she pressed a hand to her brow and fell in a dead faint on the forecourt. "You don't see, do you?"

Isabelle fiddled with her pearls. "I'm not sure I know what you mean, Adam," she said, a bit shakily.

"I mean you're forcing me to make a choice," Adam enlightened her, while casting another glance at me. He was trying to keep his voice down, I could see, but I could hear him quite clearly. "Trust me, Mom," he went on, "that is *not* something you want to do."

With which, he raked his hand frustratedly through his hair, and walked away.

I blinked in astonishment, looking from him as he came toward me, to HRH, who went a bit wilty, then turned to limp to the entrance.

Adam smiled when he reached me, a sad little smile that didn't quite reach his eyes. "You okay?" he asked.

"Yes, fine," I assured him, hoisting up my shoulders. *Better now you've shown you're still my white knight in blue... green.* "Is she?" I nodded toward his mom, who now had a pronounced dip to her walk, her crutch clacking demonstratively on the tarmac.

"She'll be all right. She's a tough old bag, despite the theatricals." He sighed, running his hand over his neck.

I supposed. Nevertheless, it was quite clear we couldn't just go and leave her to it. I was here, so I ought to get on — and prove I could never live up to Adam's perfect, culinary-gifted wife.

"I'd better get the show on the road," I said, offering him an apologetic smile regarding his *Green-Soup*-spattered predicament. "I'll take these in and come back for the tureen." Which was now half empty.

I reached for my food boxes, wherein was the *Faith in Salad*, *Drunken Chicken* and Adam's *White Soup* — carefully sealed, the *Chockfull of Zucchinis* and *Olivia's Pride*, hopefully more intact than I felt.

"I'll bring them," Adam offered. "Look, Lisa..." He placed his hand over mine, sending a spark of electricity from my nose to my toes. Did he know he did? I looked nervously at him.

"I'm sorry... about my mother," he said, with an awkward shrug.

Oh. I straightened up. "It's okay. I'm sure she doesn't mean..."

"It's not okay, Lisa. She's being a cow," Adam said bluntly.

Well yes...

"It's just..." Now he looked really awkward. He searched my face, as if gauging what my reaction might be, and then tugged in a breath. "To be honest, I think she misses Melissa, too. She doesn't actually say so, but..."

Hardly daring to breathe, I waited, not sure I wanted to hear more about how perfect Melissa was, which she obviously was to rank so high in his mother's affections.

"Mel... Melissa..." Adam stumbled on, obviously struggling for the right words "... she was a friend to Mom, you know, when Dad went. Mom was lonely and Mel felt sorry for her, and..." He shrugged again and trailed off.

Well that made sense, I supposed, which made Melissa very special, I also supposed. I'm not sure I would have been big enough to be a friend to his Mom, though I couldn't help but feel a growing smidgeon of sympathy for her. She obviously was lonely. Scared I was going to whisk Adam out of her life, probably. Poor Adam; I hadn't realized. "Did he...?" I wasn't sure how to ask. "Your dad, did he, um...?"

"Oh, no." Adam got the gist. "He came out of the closet."

"Ahhh..." My eyes shot wide. ...*gosh*. Poor Isabelle!

"Kept going, fortunately for him." Adam's mouth twitched into a smile.

"Oops." My mouth followed suit, which was entirely Adam's fault. I doubted it was very funny for his mom.

"He's always been around when I've needed him though. She's never had to scrimp and save, not really. She is lonely though, so... I put up with her... for now."

"That's because you're nice." I pressed a hand to his cheek, so wishing I could press my lips against his instead, stuff my tongue in his mouth, rip his shirt open and ravish him. If only things weren't so peculiar between us.

"I should go," I said, smiling bravely, despite my heart bleeding steadily into my tummy.

He smiled and nodded, and caught my arm as I turned. "Lisa," he said, his eyes uncertain, but firm on mine. "I know we've argued, sort of." He furrowed his brow. "And I know we're supposed to be meeting up later, but..."

Supposed to be? "But what?" I swallowed.

"... I, erm, just wanted to tell you that I..."

"Luc... a," Isabelle called from the door, "do make sure to bring the food around the back, won't you? It will make an awful mess in the foyer. Captain Summers is just coming to lend you a hand."

"*Christ!*" Adam eyed the skies. "Now, she really *has* to be joking."

Chapter 12 Love Conquers All

"Lisa, I love you." I practiced in the hall mirror as I walked through my front door, decided I looked like a fool and walked on up the hall.

Jesus, three words, "I love you!" and every time I tried to say them, I tied my frickin' tongue in a knot. Idiot was about right. A schoolkid could do better.

"Talk to her, everyone says. Tell her," I muttered to myself as I tugged off my jacket, eau-de-dog-piddle mixed with *Green Soup* possibly being a bit of a turn off, if I did ever manage to get the words out of my mouth.

So what if I did, and Lisa came back with, *I like you, but...*? I'd be a man about it, obviously. Hide the fact that my heart just got broken all over again. Tell her? Yeah, right. I yanked off my also iffy shirt. Like it *wasn't* frickin' rocket science.

Get her attention with a romantic gesture, Becky had said. I pondered as I half-ran, half-hobbled upstairs to tug on a clean shirt. Like what, exactly? The florists would be shut, and I doubted flowers from the local garage would be very romantic somehow.

Chocolates possibly? Yeah, excellent idea. Make way for the world's biggest original thinker. So what *did* I do? Racking my brains, I headed back down to pick up the *Chilli Peppers* and *Zebra* from the fridge.

"Squa*awk*. Teller. Caw, caw." Flint piped up on cue from the living room.

"Yeah, yeah. Heard that one, Flint. Thanks all the same." I reached for a cookie from the jar en route, in serious danger of starving to death, ironically.

"Squa*awwk*, tell..."

"Flint! Zip it, or..."

"*eBay. Caw, caw.*"

"Got it in one." I smiled, idly wondering whether people did actually sell parrots on eBay. Not that I would.

Right, the *Chilli Peppers* looked okay. All Lisa had to do was wham them in the oven for fifteen minutes. Oh, and sprinkle the shallot and cheese over. I grabbed up my pre-prepared pots of those, glad I'd remembered and at least got something right.

The *Zebra* looked... stripy... which was about how it should look, I supposed. Nothing much Lisa had to do with that, apart from decorating it with... "*Sh...ooot*! The Oreos!" I spat the last one out of my mouth, as if that would help.

Dammit, looked like I'd have to dive into the supermarket after all. Who knew, I might even get inspired. Yeah, right. The way to a girl's heart, a pound of sausages and a frozen chicken. I didn't think so.

Bagging up my stuff, I headed fast to the front door, practicing on the way. "Lisa, the first time I saw your smile, I realized I loved..." No. Too... convoluted "Lisa, you complete me." Reasonable, but the actual word was important, wasn't it?

Come on. Ferchrissakess, how hard could it be? Okay, so... I plucked up my keys — plonked them down and re-buttoned my shirt, correctly — then sucked in a breath and tried again... "Lisa, I..."

"*Love you. Caw, caw.*"

"eBay, definitely."

"Receiving, over," I whispered to Becky, as Her Maj wafted past behind me, her limp not quite so obviously in evidence, I noted.

"Lisa," Becky sighed, "it's a hands-free, not a walkie-talkie."

"I know," I said, watching as Isabelle slipped rather deftly into the dining area, "but we need a signal so we know... hold on." I waited while Isabelle's hand reappeared around the doorframe, groped for her wall-parked crutch, then disappeared again. "So we know when we can talk. Over means it's safe to. Out means she's come back in, and um..."

"Roger means received and understood?" Becky suggested, amused.

"No, no, *copy* means received and understood. Roger or wilco means will comply."

"Copy," Becky quipped in militaristic tones. "Roger."

"Perfect." I adjusted my hands-free under my cook's hat, my eyes sliding left and right for signs of Isabelle's eyes appearing around the doorframe to catch me cheating red-handed.

"Right, we're on our way there," Becky went on. "We'll start with the *Frisian Anchor*. You have all the ingredients, right?"

"Affirmative." I nodded, then nudged up my hat, all the better to actually see the ingredients.

"Lisa..." Becky's emitted another tolerant sigh "... I know you're trying to sound keen, sweetie, but without wishing to dampen your enthusiasm, do you think we could use the walkie-talkie jargon only when strictly necessary?"

"Roger."

"Thank you," Becky said flatly. "So, list what you have and I'll check it off against my list."

"Copy." Trying to muster up any enthusiasm at all, I searched for my recipe. Tomorrow all this will be over, I told myself brightly. Nothing but a distant, bad memory. Then remembered tomorrow Adam and I might also be over. "*Frisian Anchor*," I read, fizzling a bit.

"Ingredients?" Becky asked. "If you're missing something, we can stop on the way."

"Rambo," I replied miserably, definitely missing something. My loyal, midget Jack Russell and best furry friend ever.

"Oh, God, honestly, Lisa, you are hopeless," Becky muttered. "You must be the only person in the world who gets withdrawal symptoms from her dog. Rambo, say hello to Mommy."

"Rambo?" My dwindling spirits lifted.

"*Rrrrowf!*" Rambo answered, cute as ever with his intuitive little spots. "But..." I waited while distant scuffles subsided and Becky came back on the phone "... Her Maj will have apoplexy." She would, too. I wasn't sure Isabelle had got over the shock of Rambo peeing in her face, albeit there was pane of glass between her and his willy. Lord knew what she'd do if he pee'd on the surgically clean floor of the golf club kitchen.

"It was either bring him or leave him in the mop bucket," Becky informed me. "Fireworks going off next door. Rambo wasn't overly impressed."

"*What?!*" My poor baby had nearly drowned himself?!

"He's fine. Everything in working order, unfortunately. Fortunately, Luke has a spare pair of jeans in his backpack."

Thank God. I stopped halfway out of my pinny and hat. "Thanks, Becks," I said gratefully. "You're the best."

"I know," Becky assured me. "So, shall we get on with the *Frisian Anchor* before we actually arrive?"

"Right, yes, copy, roger."

"Yes, m'dear?" Captain Summers boomed behind me.

Eeek! "Out." I squeaked, noting he had Royal company.

Becky went quiet, then, "I take it she's back?"

"Come on... *out!*" I said, making a great show of tugging berries and red wine from my shopping bag.

"*Ahh*, copy," said Becky. "Okay, so I'll read the ingredients. You just say yes... roger, whatever... at the end, or say what you haven't got. Okay?"

"Copy. Ahem, copy? Copy...?" I knitted my brow and ferreted around the working surface as HRH came across to peer down her snooty nose over my shoulder. "Ah, got it!" Seizing on the recipe, I plucked it up, furrowing my brow further as I perused it.

"Here we go then," Becky started, "Frisian Anchor," and read the ingredients to me.

"Uh, huh," I said, as Becky paused.

"Sorry, Luce... a?" Her Maj said, eyes on the *Drunken Chicken* and hearing like radar.

"Ahem." I coughed. Please don't look in the *Green Soup* bowl, I prayed, sure that there would be a white sphere-shaped squeaky floating atop it. "Ahem, ahem, ahem."

Her Maj looked from the chicken to me. "Problem, dear?" she asked, perplexedly.

"Bit of asthma," I croaked. "Nothing to worry about."

"Oh." Isabelle looked momentarily perturbed, then, "Well, do try not to cough over the food, won't you? It's very unhygienic."

"The absolute cow!" Becky gasped, as HRH went off for a critical perusal of *Olivia's Pride*. "Tell her where to shove her do, I would."

"Roger," I growled, at which Captain Summers saluted and said, "At you service, m'dear."

Oh, God. I eyed his medal-bedecked chest and my shoulders deflated. Things in the kitchen, I suspected, were going to get awfully complicated. "Right, I'll just get on and cook the *Frisian Anchor*," I said, trying to sound chirpy, as Isabelle peered nosily in the *White Soup* bowl.

"You must be mad," Becky imparted.

Oh I'm getting there I thought, growing seriously peeved.

"But still determined, obviously, so, here we go... the cooking instructions."

Glug, glug...

"Cheers. Enjoy, hon. Have one for me." ... *glug.*

Frisian Anchor

Ingredients for 4 portions:

4 cups berries

1 cup red wine

4 tbsp sugar

1 tbsp starch (potato or corn starch)

Vanilla sauce

4 basil leaves

Cooking instructions:

Bring the wine to a boil with the sugar.

Take a few tablespoons out and mix this with the starch.

Mix the starch goo into the cooking wine and add the berries.

Bring this to a boil again, then immediately take it off the heat.

Serve in decorative bowls with vanilla sauce or vanilla ice cream and decorate with one basil leaf each.

"We're here." Becky crackled in my ear as I edged toward the *Green Soup*, intending to have a surreptitious fish around. "Meet us out back."

"I can't." I whispered as Captain Summers wandered back in, cheeks a bit rosier, his frequent trips to the kitchen being to take a quick sip from his hipflask. "Her Maj keeps flitting in and out to make sure everything's up to scratch, and the back entrance leads straight to the kitchen."

I glanced toward the door to the dining area, the porthole through which I could see Isabelle peering indiscreetly back. "Honestly, what does she think I'm going to do, spit in the chicken?"

"In her eye, you mean," Becky muttered. "Frosty old bag."

"Her Maj, the ice queen." I tittered.

"Harrumph, got you talking to yourself now, has she, m'dear?" The captain asked, meandering over, a noticeable sway to his walk. "A little something to take the chill orf?"

Oops. He'd heard, I gleaned, as he offered me his hipflask.

"Can be a bit of a handful, can't she, our Isabelle? Lonely, I reckon. Might warm up a bit, though, don't y'think?" He twirled his moustache contemplatively. "Given the right approach."

Gosh, he fancied his chances — with Isabelle? In which case, he would certainly need some liquid courage. "Possibly." I smiled, took a swig of brandy, and handed his flask back.

"Might be worth a shot, hey what?" He took another huge slug, puffed up his chest and sauntered toward the dining room door.

"What's happening?" Becky whispered.

"The captain," I whispered back, watching on as Captain Summers addressed Isabelle and got an icy glare for his efforts. "He's attempting a thaw."

"Brave man," said Becky. "Hope he doesn't get frostbite. Talking of which, where do you want us? It's really freezing out here."

Hell. Where, with Her Maj on sentry duty? I looked around panicky, then had an inspired idea. "The toilet!"

"Er..." Becky didn't sound too sure.

"They have windows. And the food's all sealed, isn't it?"

Becky sighed again, resignedly. "Okay. I'll meet you outside the window in five."

"Lisa!" Becky hissed. I flapped the window open and squeezed my head out, feet balancing precariously on the toilet seat. "Lisa, wrong window!"

Ooh! I twisted my head sideways. "Ouch!" It's you who's got the wrong window! That's the men's room."

"Whoops." Becky gathered up her baggage. "On my way. Hang on."

I didn't have much choice, did I? "Hurry up," I said, having a minor panic as I realized I might be in danger of decapitating myself if my foot slipped.

Gingerly, I tried to twist my head back, and... *ooh, er. Shu... gar!!* "Becky," I had a major panic attack, "hurry up!"

"I'm trying." Becky clip-clopped toward me on vertiginous heels, Greek God close behind, hands full of food and eyes on her butt.

"Well, come on then." She jiggled impatiently outside the window. "What are you waiting for?"

"Salvation," I wailed — quietly. "I'm stuck."

"You're... *what?!*" Becky's eyes boggled. "Oh, *wonderful*. And here comes the cavalry, not." She folded her arms as a patrol car cruised into the parking lot, blue- ights sweeping the building.

"Well done, Einstein," she muttered, marching across as Adam climbed out of the passenger side. "When I said blue lights, I meant you to attract Lisa's attention, not the entire membership of the golf club!"

"Shhhhh," I said from my vantage point, worried that that's exactly what they would do.

Adam pushed his cap back, and walked across to me, looking puzzled. "Lisa," he cocked his head to one side, "what are you doing?"

"Admiring the view." I sniffled, my bottom lip a bit wobbly.

"She's stuck," Luke supplied, while I wondered if he couldn't do something a little more helpful. Like provide a tissue and wipe my nose.

"*Jesus.*" Adam eyed the skies, which did nothing for my fast-flagging confidence. "Stay there."

"Such a wit." Becky scowled after him as he headed for the back entrance.

Hoping there was no one else in there, I located the ladies' room and went in fast as I heard a clunk from inside. "Lisa!" I called, banging the cubicle doors wide, bar one, which was locked. *Great.*

"In here," Lisa said, sounding a bit strangled. "I lost my shoe."

Realizing that had nothing to do with women's obsession with foot fashion, I was in the next cubicle and over the wall in two seconds flat, panic knotting my stomach as I noted the shoe on the floor, meaning Lisa was on tiptoe on one foot, the other foot way too close to the edge. *Christ,* what was she doing?

"It's okay," I assured her, wrapping a hand around her waist and taking her weight. "I've got you."

"My neck hurts," she muffled.

"It would." I tried to sound calm — as if standing in toilets with my cheek pressed to women's bottoms was the sort of thing I did every day. "Lisa, I'm going to climb up behind you," I told her, sliding the latch on the door should the rescue services need to gain entry. "I'll do it slowly, and I won't let go of you, okay?"

"Promise you won't?" Lisa sounded panicky.

"Never," I promised, and wished she knew how much I meant it.

It wasn't an easy maneuver, keeping one arm around her and levering myself up with the other. One slip and she could... *Jesus,* I couldn't bear thinking about it.

"Right, I've got you. Now, I'm going to slide my hand through the window and see if I can free you. Are you all right with that?"

"Uh, huh," she said. "I think so."

"Okay, so..." I had a quick recon of the situation "... I'm just going to remove your hands-free, and then I want you to turn your head — slowly — to the right. Stop if it hurts. We'll get you out, don't worry."

"Nearly there. Yep, almost. Excellent!" I sighed with relief as Lisa popped free. "Well done."

"Oh, God!" She heaved out a sob, and another. "I thought I was going to die!"

"Shhhh. You're okay. I've got you." My heart hammering, I folded her into my arms and tried to comfort her. *Hell,* she was crying. I pressed my face close to hers, breathed deep the intoxicating scent of her, and...

"... *shit,*" closed my eyes as the cubicle door flew open.

"*Oh, mon Dieu*!! Adam!" Mom gasped. "What are you doing?! And in your uniform!?"

"Be quiet, Mom, please." I stepped down, glancing at Mom as I did, who was clutching the door frame, looking about fit to pass out. *Quelle Surprise.* Ignoring her, I turned my attention back to Lisa, hitching my hands under her arms to swing her down by my side.

"Well, really...!" Mom blustered behind me. "I'm shocked, Adam. Utterly appalled. I might have known, of course. I suppose *she*..." she paused to look Lisa disparagingly up and down, "thought it was a very clever idea, trying to compromise you..."

"Cut it out, Mom!" I grated angrily. "That's enough!"

"I beg your pardon?" Mom paled and swayed.

"I said enough, Mom. Just... get out! Okay!?"

Mom backed off, sensibly. I was in danger of saying a whole lot more. Ignoring her now grasping the sink for support, I retrieved Lisa's shoe, and placed it on her foot. Then I stood up to wrap an arm around her and guide her out, daring my mother to cast so much as a glance at her as I did.

I loved him, absolutely. And I couldn't even look at him, so utterly humiliated was I — for Adam. "Thank you," I said, my eyes fixed on his lovely firm chest. I'd felt his heartbeat as he'd held me, thudding in tandem with mine.

"No problem," Adam said. "I'm good with damsels in distress."

I smiled, a bit feebly, then... *ooh, flip*... remembered another damsel who would be very much in distress, outside in the freezing cold. "Becky," I said, "I'd better let her in." I turned away, promising myself that whatever Adam had to say when we talked, I wouldn't compromise him; no tears, no demanding to know why — even if my world fell apart because he did say goodbye.

"Lisa..." Adam caught my arm.

"Yes?" I turned to look into his liquid brown eyes, so full of uncertainty.

"I, erm..." He ran a hand awkwardly over his neck. "Nothing," he said. "It can wait. Later, yes?"

"Yes." I managed a smile, despite my heart plummeting into my tummy.

He trailed a thumb across my cheek. "Mascara," he said.

"Thank you." I dredged up another smile, then dashed back to the kitchen before I ended up doing what I'd just promised myself not to.

Becky had already been granted entry, amazingly. "Lisa! Sweetie!" She flew across the kitchen to squish me in a hug. "What were you doing, for God's sake? I almost had heart failure."

"Me too," I assured her.

"Are you all right, hon?" she asked, wiping away my excess mascara as she searched my eyes; always there when I needed her, always dependable.

Thank God for friends. "Yes." I sniffled and nodded. "I think I am now."

"And I suppose the show must go on?" she asked, with a roll of her perfectly made-up eyes.

"Uh huh, absolutely." Up went my shoulders, despite my sore neck. I might not be sassy or confident, and I certainly wasn't feeling very carefree or light-hearted, but I was determined to finish what I'd started. In any case, "I'm not letting all your hard work go to waste," I told her, reaching for my hat.

"Okay," Becky reluctantly agreed. "But I'm here now. You can tell she-witch I'm the hired help. Whatever, I'm helping."

With which she beckoned Luke and produced a banquet from her food boxes. "And before you ask," she said, unveiling her specialty, *Cassata Seduction,* which really was to die for, "Rambo's in the car. He's fine. He has his piggy for company."

"Yes," I said, swiping a teeny sample of the chocolate coating, "but he won't have much fun with it now it's squeakless, will..." *Oh, hell...* "The *Green Soup!*" I still hadn't checked it for inadvertently plopped-in objects.

I was halfway to the tureen, when... "*Aaargh!...*" there was an almighty shriek from the dining area. "It's a cat!" a female voice — with a telling French accent — screamed.

"No, it's a mouse!" a male voice picked up.

"Oh, no," Becky and I exchanged glances, "it's..."

"Superdog?" Becky suggested as something spotty and suspiciously Rambo-shaped flew through the swing-door, Her Maj in hot pursuit with Captain Summers bringing up the rear, luckily. Isabelle went a bit wilty as Rambo sniffed the table, and... *eeek!*... cocked his leg.

"A dog." She pointed shakily. "Weeing in the kitchen."

"Yes, m'dear, but it's only a little one," Captain Summers assured her, an arm creeping around her waist. "Aperitif?" He offered her his hipflask.

"No. Thank you, Roger." Isabelle gave him a look that could curdle milk, but she didn't unhitch him I noticed, as I did a circuit of the table in pursuit of my yappy Jack Russell, who obviously thought it was a jolly good game.

"Rambo, sweetie, come here," I tried in my best sweet-patient tones.

"*Rrrrowf, rrrrowf. Not likely, sweetie,*" went Rambo, under the table and out the other side.

"Rambo, come on, baby," I tried, my shoulders sagging as Her Maj rambled on about health and safety behind me. "Come walkies with Mommy, hmm?"

Wag, wag. "*Rrrowf, rrrroowf. Only if you come and get me,*" was Rambo's reply.

Ooh, flip. "Rambo! Come on, hon," I cajoled, peering upside-down under the table; desperate now, as Isabelle got into full haughty, affronted mode.

"We'll have to have the whole place fumigated," she said, partaking of an aperitif. "They may well close us down." She partook of another.

Ooh... "Rambo, *please...*" I went to his left. Rambo slipped niftily right. Becky went one way, Luke went another, and... *oh, God, no...* caught his elbow on the soup tureen as he did. Mortified, I scrunched my eyes closed as the tureen hit the floor, shooting globules of *Green Soup* high into the air.

"*Rrrowf, grrrrowf. Grrrrrr... Rrrrowf,*" went Rambo, pointy ears up in alarm, then flat-down as he turned tail, scrambling under the kitchen cart in a flash, rump and stump tucked in safely behind him.

Disaster. Total disaster. My heart sank without a trace.

"Atrocious," Isabelle commented, helpfully. "Utterly... ah, Adam, darling..."

Oh, no. I hardly dared look up as the door squeaked open.

"There's a horrible little dog running around." Isabelle went on, true to obnoxious form. "Do you think you could be an angel and help round it..."

"It's not a horrible dog, Mom. It's Rambo, as you well know," Adam cut in. "Now, would you mind being quiet for once in your life?"

He turned to me, as Isabelle staggered where she stood, then clutched the delighted captain for support.

"Sorry," Adam offered, with a contrite smile. "I went to check on him, and he must have figured you were in here. I'll try and get hold of..."

"Well!" Isabelle gathered herself, redoubtably. "I've heard everything now," she spluttered, chest puffed up like a peacock. "Melissa would never have let you talk to your mother like..."

"*Christalfrickinmighty!*" Adam swung around. "Will you just drop it, Mom?! Melissa's not here! And she was *not* perfect! You drove her crackers sometimes, insisting she was."

Isabelle clutched at her pearls, now definitely shaken.

"You drive *me* crackers," Adam went on, regardless. "No one's perfect, ferchrissakes. You're not. I'm not. Lisa's not, but I don't care, don't you get it?! I don't give a flying f... damn, if her cooking's crap."

Becky sighed audibly. "He's getting to the bit where he tells her he thinks Lisa's wonderful in a minute."

"I don't want Lisa thinking she has something to prove. She doesn't!" Adam stopped, glancing at me apologetically. "Erm, I can't cook either, if it helps."

"But...?" Isabelle glanced around at the abundance of food.

"Becky," Adam supplied. "All of this is down to her. Becky can cook, fabulously. But you see, I don't love Becky because she *can* cook, anymore than I would love Luke because he's a good photographer."

"Damn," said Luke.

"I love Lisa, no matter what."

"*Aw*, finally." Becky nudged me. "I knew he'd get there eventually."

I blinked, lost for words as Adam limped over to me. "Lisa," he ran his hand through his hair, "I love you. All of you, just as you are, with all of me." With which he ferreted down his jacket and produced...

"A banana?" Becky gawped at the gift he was proffering. "He's not serious?"

"Very, I reckon." Luke nodded toward a mouse-like snout, appearing tentatively from under the kitchen cart.

"For Rambo." Adam shrugged, embarrassed. "I was hoping he'd be okay with it if his mom loved me back... a little."

Oh... my *God!* I almost peed myself. He loves me? All of me? My heart bounced gleefully back into my chest as I threw myself bodily at him.

*Squeeeeaa*K.

"Grrrrrr. Grrrowf. Grrrrrr." Shake. *SqueeaaK, squeeaaK.* "*Rrrrowf!*"

"Rambo says yes." I panted breathily, then stuffed my tongue back in Adam's delectable mouth.

"*Ahhh*," Captain Summers sighed wistfully behind us, "love's young dream. Bet we could give them a run for their money though, hey, old thi... Good Lord! There's an eyeball floating in the soup!"

"Oh," said Isabelle. "Yes, well... don't tell everyone, Roger. Or they'll all want one."

"*Stack O' Cakes*," Adam read. "Do you reckon we can do this?" He reached for the pan.

"Um, possibly." I looked him over as he studiously studied the menu. *Mmm, yummy.* "But I'm not sure you should do it naked. It might spit..." My eyes travelled downwards "... a bit."

Adam followed my gaze. "*Ah*," he said, a twinkle in his eye as he reached for his pinny. "Better?"

I eyed the naked female now adorning his torso. The very well-endowed naked female. "Honestly? Not a lot, no." I smiled my best confident woman smile, but quickly tugged his shirt tighter over my own less abundant attributes nevertheless.

"Do you know something?" Adam asked, cocking his head to one side.

"What?" I sat on my hands, before I was tempted to button the shirt up to my skull.

Adam's mouth curved into a smile as he strolled over to me. "Yep," he said, hooking a finger over my shirt and peering down my frontage, before I could protest. "As I thought..."

"Adam!"

"... perfect. From your nose..." he looked up and planted a kiss on my nose, "... to your..."

"Adam," I glanced down to where he was playing homage to my feet, "you're... *ouch!*"

"Starving." Adam stopped nibbling on my toes. "Come on," he got to his feet and plucked up my hand, "let's create another catastrophe in the kitchen."

"Instructions," he said seriously, looking not very serious in his pinny as he handed them to me. "You read, I'll cook." That suited me just fine.

"Okay." I handed him his pan to complete his master-chef look.

Stack O' Cakes

Ingredients for 6 pancakes:

1 cup milk

2 tbsp melted butter, margarine or sunflower oil

1 egg

1 cup self-rising flour (OR 1 cup of regular flour with 2 tsp baking powder)

1 tbsp sugar

½ tsp salt

Butter or oil for cooking

Grease a small frying pan with a bit of butter or oil, and keep the butter/oil out. You'll need it later.

Whisk all the ingredients together in a big bowl until the mixture is completely smooth (no lumps).

Use the whisk to break up lumpy parts against the side of the bowl.

Turn on your stove to medium-high heat (not full) and wait until a sprinkle of water in the pan instantly boils away.

Use a soup ladle and put one ladle full of mixture into the pan. The pancake surface will start to bubble. When the bubbles are popping and the holes generally stay there, use a wooden spatula to turn the pancake over. A perfect pancake is golden-brown to brown on both sides.

Repeat until you run out of dough. The last tiny one you make is for your dog so that he doesn't get jealous.

"Um, that's no lumps, Adam." I couldn't resist.

Adam flicked me with his whisk.

"Ha, ha," I said, wiping a splotch from his shirt. "Now could you... use that to break up lumpy parts against the side of the bowl."

"Looking good," Adam said, several intact pancakes later.

"Delish," I agreed, over a tummy rumble. "We can have some of Becky's *Jammed in There* with them. Oh, by the way, the last tiny pancake is for Rambo!"

"Bull," Adam said, peering sideways at the recipe. "You're pulling my leg."

"I most certainly am not." I laughed. "It says so right here, doesn't it Rambo?"

"*Rrrrowf, rrrrowf.*" Rambo came skidding eagerly in from Adam's living room, accompanied by a metallic rattle and a bell tinkle — and a manic flapping of wings.

"*Squaawwwk! eBay!*"

"For you," Adam said, pausing inbetween the mouthfuls he was feeding me to pass me a beautifully wrapped gift. Bless him. Love him.

It was a sign, I thought, replete in every sense of the word. Great minds... we were meant to be. Had to be. Bashfully, I passed him my similarly wrapped gift, hoping he wouldn't be offended. The pancakes were truly yummy.

Casting curious looks at each other, we tore off the wrapping and...

"Oh." He laughed. Thank God. I smiled. *"For Those About To Cook."* We both read, then, "I love you," we both said together.

Our eyes met, Adam's sultry, chocolaty brown eyes drinking in mine.

Our hands met, fingers entwined.

Our lips... almost met.

Rrrring, rrrring went Adam's phone.

"Ignore it," he said, huskily, his mouth a heartbeat from mine.

Rrrring, rrrring.

"I am," I said gulpily.

Rrrring... click. "Hi, lover boy." Becky oozed sexily over the voicemail, then tittered, and waited. "Well, you're obviously not there. Never mind. I just wanted to say well done on finding your kahunas, eventually. I'm not sure a banana would have been my idea of a romantic gesture, but it certainly got Lisa's attention. *Soooo*, when you get around to asking her the crucial question, some time, preferably before you both die of old age, I've got a little plan..."

"Sorry, Becks." Adam nudged the volume down as we passed on the way to the bedroom. "We have plans of our own."

Contents

Chapter 1 Faith in Salad	1
Faith in Salad	12
Chapter 2 Spice up Your Love Life	15
Chilli Peppers	24
Chapter 3 Menu Fit for a Queen	26
The Plan	28
Red Soup	35
Chapter 4 Anything for Love	38
Cassata Seduction	43
Chapter 5 Saturday Morning Fever	49
Green Soup	51
Olivia's Pride	57
Chapter 6 Guaranteed To Make You Drool	61
Impress the In-Laws (Avocado Fudge)	65
White Soup	72
Chapter 7 Mixed Messages	74
Drunken Chicken	79
Chapter 8 Bitter Sweet Love	86
Zebra	91
Chockfull of Zucchinis	97
Chapter 9 Romance on the Rocks?	100
Peach Gobbler	106
Chapter 10 The Course of True Love	111
Pizza Cookie	115
Jammed in There	122
Chapter 11 Food for Thought	123
Cheese Cream Ahoi	129
Poseidon Serves Up	131
Chapter 12 Love Conquers All	136
Frisian Anchor	140
Stack O' Cakes	149
Acknowledgements	153

Acknowledgements

With thanks to Kim, Will and all at Safkhet Publishing for all their hard work in getting *Recipes for Disaster* out there. I was excited by Kim's inspired idea to wrap rom com around fab, fun recipes from outset. Writing the book and working with Safkhet has been an absolute pleasure from inception to publication.

I would also like to thank the fabulous cover model for being such a sport and baring his legs under his pinny for the whole world to ogle. Sexilicious! I hope he's now insured his assets.

Lastly, to Brian and Drew, thank you for supporting me, for reading my drafts, and laughing out loud when you did. Publishing a book is about much more than the actual writing.

So, here's to the team! I love it when a plan comes together.